Regina Puckett's Short Tales of Horror

REGINA PUCKETT

Regina Puckett

Without limiting the rights under copyright(s) reserved above and below, no part of this publication may be reproduced, stored in or introduced into a retrieval system, or transmitted, in any form, or by any means (electronic, mechanical, photocopying, recording, or otherwise) without the prior permission of the copyright owner.

Please Note

The scanning, uploading, and distributing of this book via the internet or via any other means without the permission of the copyright owner is illegal and punishable by law. Please purchase only authorized electronic editions, and do not participate in or encourage electronic piracy of copyrighted materials. Brief passages may be quoted for review purposes if credit is given to the copyright holder. Your support of the author's rights is appreciated.

Regina Puckett

Punk &
Sissy
Publications

Copyright © 2012 Regina Puckett

Cover Art designed by Charity Parkerson

Photographer JeffreyCollingwood/Dreamstime

Editor: Hercules Editing and Consultants

All rights reserved.

Regina Puckett

CONTENTS

1. *Mine-* A night of ghost hunting with a sexy coworker turns into a deadly game of cat and mouse with an evil spirit. Can anything save them when the spirit decides they belong to him?
2. *Crying through Plastic Eyes-*A messy divorce, a room filled with creepy dolls, and a missing six-year-old all create the perfect storm for a young mother's worse nightmare.
3. *Will Work for Food-* You see them everywhere begging for money or food. When an older couple decides to lend a helping hand to a young man and his son, someone gets more than they bargain for.
4. *Pieces-*A battered woman confesses to the mutilation and death of her husband, but did she really commit this heinous crime?
5. *Paying the Hitchhiker-*You see a beautiful young woman on the side of the road with her thumb out, asking for a ride. Who should be the most afraid: the hitchhiker or the person picking her up?
6. *Inheritance-*A confession from Accalia's grandmother about a curse and an inheritance are just the prologue to seven days of suffering through a living hell.

Regina Puckett

Regina Puckett

ACKNOWLEDGMENTS

I'm always so grateful to all of my readers. I enjoy every review and suggestion. This is an occupation that is lonely by nature so it is always welcoming to hear what others think.

Regina Puckett

Regina Puckett

MINE

Regina Puckett

Alle assessed the situation as open-mindedly as possible. She was in an abandoned mental hospital. It was pitch black and hotter than Hades. Her date was nowhere to be seen, and some people seemed to believe that this waste-littered, satanic graffiti painted dump was haunted by ghosts. While she didn't believe in ghosts, it was unnerving to be in a place that, according to rumor, was used for devil worship and animal sacrifice.

Yep. It was official. This was by far the worst first date on which she had ever been.

Her new co-worker, James, was certainly a man that was easy on the eyes. Because he had hinted all week long that they were going to be doing something really special for their first date, she had shampooed, showered, perfumed, and put a really cute, hot-pink cotton blouse. But here it was only a couple of hours into the date, and she was no longer very fresh or clean. It felt as if she

Regina Puckett

was layered from head to toe in dust and the cute blouse was completely soaked in perspiration. To think she had spent her hard earned money on new clothes and shoes to impress her now missing-in-action date. If James had been honest and told her upfront that they would be jumping over trash all night, she could have dressed accordingly. But then, what was the correct outfit to go ghost hunting in?

If they had just gone out to dinner like a normal couple, she wouldn't be lost now in a maze of darkened hallways, in a building that hadn't been hooked up to electricity in years. Of course, now probably wasn't a good time to begin thinking about food. She had been trying not to notice that her stomach had been grumbling for some time now. A few times, she had even imagined the smell of bacon and toast. If she ever saw James again, she was going to have to have a talk with him about first date protocol. The man was a clueless mess if he thought that searching through dust and mildew was going to win her heart. It might have been a completely different story if he had ever, at some point during the night, used the darkness as an opportunity to sneak in a romantic kiss, but no such luck. He had single-mindedly

Regina Puckett

searched out the spirit world with a passion she would never understand in a million years. She could only guess that he found dead people more interesting than her.

This little adventure was taking place in the middle of the hot August heat. The summer temperature had been well over a hundred degrees all day, so during the course of the late afternoon, the abandoned building had been turned into a blazing inferno. Even though it was well past midnight, the heat in the unventilated buildings had been hot enough to cause her once freshly shampooed and styled hair to become a hot mess of cobwebs, grime, and sweat. The new eighty dollar sandals were scratched and battered from tripping over loose plaster, discarded equipment, and bits and pieces of other crap that littered the floors in all of the abandoned buildings they had trekked through during the night. To make matters worse, if they could get worse, there was a good possibility that since the dilapidated hospital was so ancient, she was probably now breathing in life-endangering asbestos. On a scale of one to ten, the date was now at a minus two and falling rapidly.

As if the dirt and grime weren't bad

Regina Puckett

enough, Alle was totally lost. Since she had no idea in which direction James had wandered, she made the decision to stay where she was at and wait for him to come back and find her. All evening, she had held onto the back of his shirt, so they wouldn't become separated from each other in the dark. She had turned him loose in order to turn around and investigate a hair-raising scratching sound behind them, and when she turned back to take hold of his shirt again, he was nowhere in sight.

Since he had the only flashlight and map of all of the buildings, she leaned back against the nearest wall so nothing could sneak up behind her, and she waited. It had seemed like a good plan at the time, but the longer she stayed there, the creepier it got. After a few minutes of listening to all of the weird noises that were manifesting all around her, she erected a barrier to keep out all of the ghosts or non-ghosts alike. She pulled every piece of hospital equipment that could be rolled and stacked into a semicircle around her. If anything tried to get her, it was going to have to wade through a mass of stuff first. This helped her to feel a little safer. As soon as she had the beds in place, she plopped onto the dirty floor and waited.

Regina Puckett

While the beds probably weren't that much protection from a ghost, she felt a little safer, wedged between a moldy, mildewed wall and behind several discarded metal-framed hospital beds and filing cabinets instead of being out in there in the open where anyone or thing could get to her. Of course, with all of that hard work completed, she had nothing to do but listen to what sounded like a family of rats trying to chew through the very wall against which she was pressed. She decided to worry about the rats later, if they made it out. Her first worry was all the noises coming from the long stretches of darkened hallways. Every now and then, she would see a dark outline of something or someone move as if it was moving toward her.

Alle wasn't certain how she had gotten herself into this strange predicament. As soon as James came to pick her that evening, he had explained that they would be spending the entire night ghost hunting at the mental hospital. She should have spoken up right then and refused to go, but he had looked so cute in a worn out tee shirt and a backwards baseball hat on his head. There was no way she could refuse him anything at that point. They had spent the first part of the

Regina Puckett

night wandering around in several of the smaller buildings on the thirteen-building hospital campus, with eleven of James' ghost hunting friends, but about an hour into the hunt, everyone agreed to split into teams of twos, so they could search the buildings faster. The theory was that they wouldn't have so many distractions with less people making noise.

It had been a huge relief to Alle that they were all going their separate ways because it had been so unnerving to have a few of the others making such a big production out of every little noise they heard. At least three of James' friends would let out a loud shish and then whispered dramatically, "What in the hell was that sound?"

Since it was her first real live ghost hunt, the first thirty times of stopping and waiting to see what was creating the noises scared her witless and worried her sick about what type of faceless entity was going to come jumping out of the walls at them. Finally, a mixture of exhaustion and reason had set in and she realized that she had slipped right over the crazy hill with the rest of the nuts. It was only then the noises stopped being so unnerving and she could see the only thing in these buildings besides them were rodents and roaches.

But then, after the last forty-five minutes of being alone in the dark hallway, seeds of doubt were slowly seeping in and taking root. Maybe James didn't remember he had a date. What if in all of his excitement to capture something on his recorder, he had forgotten about her? What if she had to stay there all night?

That dreadful thought made her stomach churn into a knot of tension. "Calm down. Don't overreact." Somewhere out in the darkness and maze of buildings, James and his other like-minded, crazed ghost hunters were wandering around with cameras, tape recorders, and a bunch of other spirit-catching gadgets. Sooner or later, someone was going to remember her. "They'll come back. I know they'll come back."

With that said, Alle strained to see down the long hallway again. It was a pointless act, because all she could really see was more darkness and large looming shapes of what she dearly hoped were more pieces of hospital equipment. The sounds were the most unnerving thing to deal with alone in the dark. Every now and then, a huge chuck of plaster would fall from the ceiling and the noise would reverberate throughout the entire floor. It wasn't until she heard footsteps that she began to feel the best bit of hope that James was indeed going to remember he had a date and was returning for her.

"Hello. James is that you?" She waited but no one answered. She stopped and listened again. Without thinking, she stood up out of her crouch and peeked over the metal railing of the hospital bed. Even the rats stopped chewing and seemed to be waiting and listening for an answer.

"Look, guys. This isn't funny. I'm hot, I'm thirsty, and I'm tired. I want to go home." She stared at the dark shadow and tried to see if it was James or not, but it was too dark to make out the face. It looked to be about the right height and size of James, but the features were totally in the shadows. When no one answered her, she became even more unnerved than before. "Okay. You're really starting to creep me out. If that's you, James, this is not funny. I have to insist that you take me home."

Alle sniffed back tears. There was no way she was going to cry like some big old baby. It was a dark, scary building, so what? In the bright light

Regina Puckett

of day, it was certain to be just a dusty, old building. In just a couple of more hours, the sun would be up and if James hadn't returned by then, she would find her own way out of the building and back home. James had better hope she didn't have to that, because if she did, she was going to post messages on Facebook and Twitter, and let everyone know what a jerk he was. By the time she was finished, he would never get another date.

The damn dimple should have been a dead giveaway. She had never dated anyone with a dimple who had ever turned out to be the person he presented himself to be. Dimples were her Achilles' heel. She loved them. It didn't really matter where they were located; chin or cheeks. However, she didn't know what it was about having a dimple that turned a guy into such a total ass. Maybe it was because the dimple made them look so innocent and appealing that they could get away with murder. Most guys could do what they wanted, when they wanted, and all they had to do to get out of trouble was to grin. That dimple would come out, and all would be forgiven, but it was going to take a lot more than a cute dimple for her ever to forgive James for deserting her.

Without warning, the atmosphere in the

Regina Puckett

hallway took a dramatic change. The air around Alle felt thicker and pulsated between hot and cold. The muggy air had so much static electricity in it that every hair on her body felt as if it was standing on end. That strange sensation set her on edge, and she was unprepared when someone let out a long, slow sigh into her right ear. She could have chalked up the sigh as something out of her imagination, but there wasn't just the sound of the sigh, but a breeze that blew across the back of her neck and cheek.

Trying to keep a lid on her spiraling panic, Alle turned ever so slightly to see if someone had somehow managed to sneak up behind her. She was fairly certain there was no way anyone could be there. She was flat against the wall, and with all of the beds and equipment stacked between her and the rest of the hallway it would have taken an army and several tanks to crash through the barrack that was erected. Even knowing all of this, Alle was still relieved to turn and see nothing but the expected wall.

She whipped her head around when the sound of footsteps started all over again. This time there was the barest hint of movement. She could have sworn she saw the shape of a man before it disappeared back into the dark hallway again.

Alle tried to remain calm, but her voice came out as a high pitched squeal. "I don't know who it is that's playing games with me, but this is not funny."

Still, no one answered. She shoved the bed that was directly in front of her out of the way and marched in the direction of the footsteps. "James! Is that you?" She stopped for a moment and listened. This time she spoke more to herself than to anyone who might be listening. "I just want to go home. Please. I just want to go home."

Alle lifted her chin and steeled up some courage for the long trip down the dark hallway. She actually made it several steps before all of her forced bravo evaporated. It felt as if she walked into the middle of a large spider web. She hated spiders and their webs. She stopped and wiped furiously at where it felt like the webs were, but no matter how hard she tried to get them off, she couldn't find any trace of the cobwebs.

While she was busy trying to figure out why she couldn't find any of the web on her face, the air around her went crazy again. It went from

Regina Puckett

humid and hot to bone chilling cold in the matter of seconds. She stifled a whimper and flattened up against the hallway wall. She held her breath and waited. Her arms had the strange sensations that the hairs were standing up on them again, so she rubbed her forearms and tried not to panic. Just when it seemed as if the air was settling back to normal, there came another long sigh, but this time it was followed with what felt like a finger sliding across the edge of her chin and down the base of her throat.

She flayed out both arms in an attempt to hit whoever was toying with her, but no matter in which direction she struck out, she couldn't make contact with anything or anyone.

"Stop it! Stop it! Stop it!" The words might have made more of an impact if she hadn't been sobbing. The fright and frustration made her feel bone weary, so when she was finally able to calm down, she decided the only thing to do was to try and find the door to the stairwell. It seemed like the wisest course of action was just to continue down the hallway. She had to stumble upon an exit sooner or later. There had to be several ways out the building. She would search and search until she found a way that headed down and out. There was absolutely no doubt in her mind now that if she didn't find James by the time she was out of the building, she was going to walk all the way home. She couldn't bear the thought of staying any longer than necessary in this spooky place.

Alle spotted an exit sign just as the odd aroma hit her senses. She stopped because the smell was so out of place in the damp, musty building. It was the strange, pungent scent of whiskey and cigars. That scent might have been comforting in another place and time. However, since it was so out of place in the deserted hospital, it only caused her more unease. She didn't stand still for very long. It only took her a moment to label what she thought the scents were, and as soon as she had that settled in her mind, she made a dash toward the stairway exit.

The moment the door to the stairway clicked shut behind her, she panicked, because the stairwell was even darker than the hallway had been. She stood and took in several long breaths, and used that time to get adjusted to the difference in the light. She moved cautiously toward the stair railing and felt better once she had a hold of it. She figured she could use it to feel her way the rest of the way down the stairs. The steps were made of concrete so she didn't have to worry about them being damaged from old age.

Just being in the stairwell gave her hope that she was going to be out of the building soon. She felt certain that she could find her way off of the hospital property once she was outside. There was a full moon tonight so there was plenty of light outside, and even though she wasn't certain about the time, it had to be getting close to sunrise.

Alle gripped the railing for all it was worth and began the long climb down the stairwell. She moved cautiously since there was so little light in the closed off area, but with each step she took, her mood brightened. This night was soon going to be just a bad memory. She truly hoped that James was okay. It worried her that he hadn't tried to find her again as soon as he realized they had become separated. There were so many dangerous areas in the dilapidated buildings. She hoped he wasn't laying somewhere in there hurt, without a way to tell anyone. They had discovered almost immediately that because of the thick concrete walls and floors, their cell phones were useless.

Alle would try calling James once she was

outside. There wouldn't be anything blocking phone service out there. If nothing else, surely some of the others were finished searching the building to which they had been assigned. If no one else were out there, she would call the police and send out a search party to locate James and make sure he was okay. She was way past the point of caring whether such a thing would embarrass him or not. This first date was going to be their only date. There was nothing wrong with him doing this sort of thing in his spare time, but that didn't mean she would be spending any more time in a strange or deserted building again.

With her thoughts so focused, it didn't register that the next landing was better lit than the one on which she was. When she finally noticed the extra light, she rushed down the steps between the two landings and found a discarded flashlight. To whom could it belong? She wasn't going to look a gift horse in the mouth so she picked it up. Now she wouldn't have to worry so much about each step.

The flashlight was a welcome addition to her downward journey, because of not only the light, but the weight of it made her feel a little safer too. Now if someone jumped out at her, she had something to hit them with. Not that she really expected anyone to jump out at her, but she was armed all the same. She had so much pent up nervous energy, she could probably tackle a water buffalo and win.

That silly thought made her giggle. The happy little sound echoed off the concrete walls and bounced back around to her. The echo bolstered her spirits for about three seconds and then the static hot and cold air enveloped her again. This time the air was so intense and thick that it caused her to gag and become lightheaded. The feeling became so bad, she collapsed onto the nearest step and drew in several deep breaths in an attempt to keep from throwing up. She was almost feeling normal again, when the sigh came. She immediately jumped up in an attempt to get away from what she was certain was going to happen next, but she wasn't fast enough.

This time, the touch was not a gentle caress, but felt as if someone was raking their fingernails across the side of her cheek. The pain was immediate and very intense. She took off running down the stairway and was able to make it down two whole sections before she stumbled and fell. The fall wasn't as bad as it could have been since she was almost to the last step and only lunged a few feet forward into the concrete wall of the next landing. Her forehead took most of the damage. For a brief moment, she saw a combination of red and yellow lights flashing before her eyes.

Alle rubbed her head and tried to regain control over her emotions. Whatever was trying to scare her was doing an excellent job. She could let this bully win or she could get out of there before something really bad happened. She didn't believe in ghosts, so whatever was happening had to be some bad practical joke gone horribly wrong. This had better not be James' idea of a fun date.

She quietly assessed her injuries. Her head hurt and she was fairly certain her big toe was broken from stubbing it on the crack in the cement step. "But you're still alive and a little wiser." She wasn't going to let whoever was tormenting her get the upper hand again. She was going to continue the downward trip to the first floor. She had to be at least halfway down by now. Just a few more minutes and she would be outside. There wouldn't be any stopping her then. She would run home if it came to that.

Regina Puckett

Alle directed the flashlight's beam toward the direction from which she had just fallen. There was nothing to see, but it had occurred to her that one of the ghost hunting bunch was following her. She didn't see anything up the steps, but she saw something hanging from the railing of the upper platform. She swung the beam in that direction and screamed. In her panic, she dropped the flashlight. It clattered and rolled up against the bottom step before stopping.

"Oh my God! Oh my God! Oh my God!" she prayed and ran as fast as her legs would take her down the remaining sets of landings and steps. The flight response had been too great to even consider anything else but getting out of the hospital. By some miracle, she made it to the ground floor without falling again. The moment she pushed the stairwell door open, she saw moonlight shining through a set of double doors. She ran across the large lobby and was relieved to find that the doors had push bars on them so no one could be trapped in the building in case of a fire. She slammed through one of the doors and took the steps leading away from the building two at a time.

Even after she was off of the steps, Alle

didn't stop running. She ran out toward the circular drive and continued running in small circles, looking around at the surrounding building with the hope that some of the others would be out there. When she did not see anyone, she finally stopped. She leaned forward and placed both hands on her knees. She pulled in long draws of air, trying to catch her breath and slow her heart rate down. When she finally had her breathing somewhat under control, she placed a call to 911 operator.

"I need an ambulance and the police!"

It was reassuring to hear a calmer voice on the other end. "What's the emergency and address?"

The images of the swinging body hanging from the stairwell landing flashed as if from a badly crafted horror movie. "He's dead! James is dead! He's hanging in the stairwell!" The tears came then. She couldn't talk because she was hiccupping.

"Miss, you're going to have to calm down. What's the address? I can't send anyone out there until I have the address."

Regina Puckett

Alle sniffed and hiccupped a few more times before she said anything else. "I came with a local ghost hunting group. I don't know the exact address but we're all at the old deserted mental hospital. James said they had a permit to be here. I don't know where everyone else is. We all broke up into different group earlier and I haven't seen them in hours."

Alle waited and listened while the operator tapped onto a keyboard.

"I've contacted the sheriff and the EMTs. Stay where you are and wait. Someone will be there shortly."

Alle's biggest fear was that the operator was going to hang up and she was going to be alone again. "Please stay on the line with me. I'm afraid. Something bad is here. I don't know who or what it is but there's evil everywhere."

For a moment, Alle thought the operator had hung up but the lady spoke again. "I'm not going any place. What's your name?"

She let out a long sigh and tried to suppress a hiccup but with only limited success. "It's Alle. Alle Greene."

Regina Puckett

The 911 operator stayed on the phone until the sheriff arrived. He turned out to be a huge, bald guy who didn't blink the entire time she was explaining the reason for being in the deserted mental hospital complex that time of night. It didn't take a rocket scientist to see from his expression that he didn't think much of people who ran around deserted buildings looking for ghosts, but he was professional enough not to express any of those thoughts out loud.

The EMTs arrived moments later, but the sheriff made the two men wait in the ambulance until the building could be secured. He locked Alle in the back of the patrol car with the explanation that she would be safer there. He did manage not to sound so stern when he suggested that she use this time to rest. He slammed the car door shut, and then disappeared into building from which Alle had worked so hard to escape.

She was extremely uncomfortable, locked in the backseat of the patrol car. The smell was awful. It was a strange combination of vomit, old sweat and a more recent addition of a flowery air freshener. Everything about the backseat area was repugnant, so instead of leaning back and relaxing, she sat forward and grasped both knees in order to keep from touching the seat or surrounding areas.

It was very unnerving, the way the EMT attendants continued to glance over at her, as if they were worried she was someone about which to be concerned. What did they think she was going to do, break out of the sheriff's car and attack them or something? It was a big relief when the sheriff finally came back out. He walked directly over to the two attendants and motioned for them to go ahead and get out of the ambulance. As soon as they joined him, the sheriff glanced over at her. She hoped he would come over and tell her that James wasn't dead and that someone had been playing a terrible trick on her, but instead he simply turned back toward the building. The other two men followed.

While it had been uncomfortable sitting in the back of the car when the sheriff was in the building before, it was now very unnerving to be out there alone again. Every now and then, she thought she could smell the scent of whiskey and cigars again, but she chalked it up to her imagination working overtime. Since there was no escaping the sheriff's car, she felt like a sitting duck. Where was the rest of James' group? Had they already left and gone home? It didn't make any sense that none of them had appeared the entire time she had been sitting there.

A quick peek at the sky revealed that it was gradually turning lighter. It was going to be a gray, misty morning, but at least it was soon going to be daylight. She looked around and wondered why none of the others had emerged yet. Some of them should have already finished and been ready to go home by this time. There was nothing that interesting in the old building to have kept them that occupied. While she was staring out the front windshield, she caught a glimpse of several sets of headlights and blue lights pulling into the drive behind the sheriff's car.

Eight patrol cars parked next to and behind the sheriff's car. Officers climbed out and hurried toward the front entrance of the main building. They waited there until the sheriff came out. When he did, he made several gestures toward each of the remaining buildings. After listening intently, the officers immediately grouped into pairs and took off in a fast jog to their assigned areas. When they had all left, the sheriff pulled out a cell phone and spoke into it for what seemed like an eternity. As soon as he finished that conversation, he looked out toward Alle. They stared at each other for an uncomfortable amount of time before he headed toward the car.

She dearly hoped the sheriff was going to let her out. The smell was really becoming overpowering and she needed a little fresh air, but those hopes were dashed when he slid into the front seat without even looking at her.

"Could you let me out for a little while? It is really stuffy in here."

Their eyes met in the mirror. There was coldness in his expression that shot a shiver down her spine. His shook his head and then broke eye contact with her. "No can do. You're taking a little trip down to the station. I still have several questions about what happened out here last night. Several things don't add up."

Before Alle could question what didn't add up for him, the hand held radio on his belt filled the car with several static filled messages for the sheriff to get over to Buildings C and D. She sat there in stunned silence. What had the other officers so upset? She sat there another thirty minutes, wondering what was taking place. While she waited, more vehicles pulled onto the hospital grounds. A couple of the cars were the sheriff's deputies and the rest of the patrol cars looked to be from the surrounding counties. The last vehicle to pull up was from the Coroner's office. None of these officers paid any attention to Alle. They huddled in deep discussion for several minutes before scurrying off into different directions.

After a while, it all became too much to handle. Exhaustion finally won out over being grossed out by the condition of the backseat. She sat back and closed her eyes.

She wasn't awoken by the long sigh, but the stinging pain on her stomach and the low whisper that sounded very much like "*Mine.*" The sound and the pain made her shoot straight up and bang her face on the wire cage separating the back and front seats.

The pain was so intense, she pulled the pink blouse up high enough so that part of her lacy bra showed. At first, there was nothing to see, but then three long welts appeared. They ran from the top of her navel to the edge of her pale blue, bikini panties. Parts of the wounds were so deep that blood began to seep out. Alle scooted over to one of the side windows and began beating on the glass.

"Get me out of here! Get me out of here!"

There was no one in sight, but that didn't stop her from screaming and beating on the glass trying, to get someone's attention. Somewhere in the back of her panicked brain, it registered that the air had begun to turn heavier and was now chilly enough so that she could see her breath as she screamed. Then the scent of vomit was replaced with the sharp smell of smoke.

Alle closed her eyes and began to pray. There was a presence now in the car with her. She had an eerie sensation of someone almost close enough to touch her, but they weren't. She was steeling up the nerve to turn around, when the sound of someone tapping on the window startled her. She let out a squeal and was ready to scream again. When she opened her eyes, she saw the sheriff leaning forward and looking in at her.

She pounded on the window and screamed. "Get me out of here! Get me out of here now! There's something in here with me!"

He looked into the backseat behind her

Regina Puckett

and then back at her. He scratched his chin and shook his head as if he thought she might be nuts. Instead of opening the door and letting her out, he opened his door, getting into the car. He spoke over his shoulder. "I'm taking you in now. I don't know what went on out here last night. But I have twelve dead people. I don't know who was out here helping you kill these people, but you will answer all my questions when we get to the station. I'll not have any more of this ghost bullshit. You and I both know it's just a load of crap."

Alle leaned her head on the wire screen. She tried to absorb his words and their meaning. How could everyone be dead? When she was finally able to speak, she hated that her voice came our as a pathetic whimper. "Please don't leave me alone out here again. Something followed me out of that place." She pulled her blouse up to show him her stomach. "It keeps scratching me. I think it just called me, 'his.' Please help me. I don't know what happened to James and his friends. You have to believe me. I don't know anything other than I was lost and I found James' body when I was coming down the stairs."

The sheriff eyed the wounds on her

stomach and then made a disgruntled sound. "I see wounds all over you. You know what I think? I think you got them when those poor people were fighting for their lives. You really think you can convince me that those scratches were made by a ghost and those poor souls were killed by the same ghost? That insane defense doesn't usually work too well out in this neck of the woods, young lady. We may be country folks, but we're not stupid. If I were you, I would use the ride to jail to think really hard about telling me the truth. It will go a whole lot easier on you in the long run."

He stared intently at her as if that would be enough for her to see the error of her ways. He then turned back around in his seat and started the patrol car.

Sheriff Wilson stirred two more teaspoons of creamer into his cup of coffee and let out a long sigh. He had purposely left Alle in the locked interrogation room all alone, since she had pleaded so hard for him not to do so. It seemed like the most logical thing to do. If she worked herself into a big enough tizzy, she would be willing to spill her guts by the time he got back in there to her. He had pretended to forget that he had left her hands cuffed behind her back. He figured that would be degrading enough to sweeten the pot a little. She was probably ready to confess to helping to kill President Kennedy by now.

He took his time and sipped on the piping hot coffee. It had been a long night and he was ready to get the interview over with so he could go home and get a little sleep before his next evening shift came around. He waited until he had drained the last drop of coffee before heading back to the interview room. He smiled at the officer standing by the locked door.

"Any problems out of her?"

The young man shook his head. "She was crying earlier, but I haven't anything out of her in the last thirty minutes. I figure she's about ready for you so she can get out of those cuffs. The ladies sure hate being cuffed up like that."

The sheriff grinned again and nodded his head in agreement. He knocked a couple of times just to let her know that he was coming up. He wanted to give her a second or two to absorb the fact that he was going to turn her sweet little world upside down. He used the key to unlock the door. He wasn't looking up and he put the key ring into his pocket as he entered the room. When he finally did look up, it took several seconds for his brain to register the shocking sight before him.

Alle was no longer sitting in the chair in which he had placed her, but was hanging from the water pipes that ran through the ceiling to the outdated plumbing in the restroom next door. Her pink cotton shirt had been torn into long strips, then tied together to form a long length that wound around her neck and the steel pipes. Both of her hands were still handcuffed behind her. He leaned against the door frame and started to call out for the officer come help get her down, when the air turned into a heavy mist, causing his arms to break out in goose bumps and the hairs to stand straight up. While he would never admit to it later when questioned about the girl's death, he could have sworn he felt a long sigh on the back of his neck and heard one word whispered.

"*Mine.*"

The End

Regina Puckett

CRYING THROUGH PLASTIC EYES

Regina Puckett

The townhouse was way too quiet without Krissy and Sassy running from room to room giggling, barking, and playing. All of that roughhousing always created a chain reaction of floors bouncing, china rattling, and whatnots falling. It was an absolute miracle anything ever survived their cheerful games of Chase and Catch.

Looking away from the box into which she had been trying to cut, Destiny glanced toward the silent pieces of china. She hated everything about their stillness, but the solitude had been nibbling away at her insides since Friday night. She missed Krissy with every fiber of her being. With just one weekend into the divorce, it was easy to see that she wasn't going to enjoy being by herself on the days when her daughter had to stay with her father.

The only thing that had been able to keep her mind off of the much-too-quiet house had been the unending task of going through her mom's personal belongings. The remaining scattered boxes in the dining room were the last few things she needed to check through to see if any of it could be used, given, or thrown away.

Destiny focused again on the box poised between her hand and the edge of the tabletop. She sliced through the tape and then separated the lid. She gently pulled out a porcelain doll from the many layers of its thin protective tissues. Her very first reaction to the old doll was a grimace that she followed with a slow, thoughtful headshake. She stared for several seconds at the monstrosity and then placed it onto the table with the others.

After a quick survey of the odd assortment of twisted limbs and disarrayed hair, she sighed. "I have no idea what Mom was thinking when she bought so many ugly dolls." At that exact moment, the mouth of the doll nearest to her popped open unexpectedly. The click was unnaturally loud, and it freaked Destiny out so much, she stepped away from the table to distance herself from all of the staring dolls. She tried calming down by taking in a couple of deep breaths. When she was certain she wasn't going to die from a heart attack, she pointed at the cause of the scare. "I've always hated clowns. You're going to be the first thing I throw into the burning barrel when I get rid of all this mess."

Regina Puckett

The clown's mouth snapped back closed and at the same time, a cold nose pressed up against Destiny's ankle. Both incidents were so unanticipated she screeched and jumped. When she looked around, she found that the cold nose belonged to Krissy's dog, Sassy. Sassy's confused expression was enough to make Destiny giggle.

As an apology for startling the small terrier, she reached down and patted the top of the dog's head. "I didn't mean to scare you, but Creepy Clown Eyes here freaked me out just a little bit. You can help me watch it burn later, if you want to."

Sassy tilted her head and whined, so Destiny knelt and picked her up. "I miss Krissy too. It won't be like this forever. If he runs true to form, Tony will quit calling or picking her up in a couple of months. My guess is the visits won't last that long. He's just taking her now because he knows it hurts me."

The two of them stared into each other's eyes and wallowed in self-pity until they both heard the front door opening and closing.

"Mom!"

Regina Puckett

Sassy struggled until she was free. She gave a happy little yap and then ran as fast as her tiny legs would carry her toward the living room.

Destiny grinned. She knew exactly how Sassy felt. Krissy was home! She followed the excited dog into the living room and watched the happy reunion for a moment, before finally rushing over hugging her daughter. While they were in a tight embrace, the front door opened again. It was a moment or two before she looked back toward the doorway. When she did, she was surprised to find her ex with a sexy young woman. The two of them were linked arm in arm as if they were afraid someone was going to try and separate them.

Before Destiny could say anything, her ex tossed Krissy's overnight bag across the room. It landed hard up against the glass television stand and caused several DVDs to fall and crash onto the wood floor. A few of the plastic cases shattered and splintered off and went flying into several different directions.

That thoughtless act rekindled the flame of fury that her ex always managed somehow to keep lit deep inside of her. He liked getting a rise out of her so she quickly tampered down any signs of anger and plastered on a fake smile. The faster she could get him and his latest tart out of her new home, the better it would be for everyone involved. Even though Tony didn't mind fighting in front Krissy, Destiny didn't like to, so she was determined to stay pleasant and civil, even if it killed her.

To return to the earlier contented feelings, she pretended no one was there to assess and critique the happy reunion. Destiny turned and grinned at Krissy again. "Hey, Baby!"

She picked up her light-weight daughter and squeezed her just to hear her giggle. The six-year-old had the sweetest, most innocent little laugh in the world. It was heaven to hear it again after all of the earlier silence. Destiny's squeeze was rewarded with a return death- defying hug that had an added full-mouth, sloppy kiss that only a kid could get away with and have the receiver savor every second of it.

As soon as Krissy was finished with the kiss, she struggled out of Destiny's arms and picked up Sassy. That reunion had an even wetter and sloppier kiss. There was lots of tongue action on Sassy's part, but Krissy didn't seem to mind in the least. When both of them appeared to be satisfied that the other had survived the weekend and all was well, Krissy went skipping out of the room and down the hallway toward her bedroom, without a backward look at any of the grownups. Sassy ran on the back of her heels as fast as she could.

The moment they were out of sight, Tony pulled his arm out of the crook of the young woman's elbow and glared in the direction into which Krissy had disappeared. He then whipped the glare toward Destiny.

She felt the heat of his rage from across the room.

"She gets her bad manners from you. She could have at least kissed me goodbye and thanked me for all the money I had to spend on her this weekend to keep her entertained. She eats like a horse and is a spendthrift just like you are. At least I had the good sense to get rid of one of you."

The tart by Tony's side giggled. The fact that he could talk about his daughter in such a disrespectful way made Destiny see red and she could no longer control her tongue. She lodged a fist on the side of her hip and pointed a finger in his direction. "You did not get rid of me. I got rid of your philandering ass, and for your information I always brought in more money from my job then you ever did. Any money I spent was made by me. Every penny you ever made was spent on booze and your cheap whores. You might think that you're impressing this little bit of jailbait, but I can almost guarantee that if she doesn't already know that you're more talk than walk, then she soon will. Now get out of my house. Any rights you think you ever had to talk to me in that tone went when the divorce papers were signed."

For a moment, it looked as if Tony might collapse from a stroke. His eyes were budging out and his face was now a lovely shade of crimson. Destiny steeled herself and waited for the verbal attack, but before Tony could overcome the shock of Destiny's rant the girlfriend tugged on the sleeve of his shirt to get his attention. This must have reminded him that he had a witness and he needed to save whatever poison he wanted to spill out for a more private moment. He backed toward the open doorway and sent a look in Destiny's direction that left no doubt in her mind that they weren't finished with this argument.

As soon as the unwelcome company had vacated the premises, she closed and locked the door behind them. She then leaned up against it and closed her eyes. She focused on slowing her heart rate. It was too bad that divorcing someone didn't get them out of your life forever. Unfortunately, when you had a child together the only benefit in getting a divorce was that you had a longer amount of time to regroup and reload ammunition.

A shrill scream forced Destiny's eyes back open and sent her heart racing.

"Mom!"

In a panic, Destiny took off running in the direction of the scream, only to find Krissy in the dining room with the table full of dolls.

Krissy was holding one up and smiling. The smile on her daughter's face was the only thing that made her switch down from "panic" mode to the lower level of "confused" mode. She should have already grown used to the fact that children could scream as if someone was trying to kill them only to discover, after running to what you thought was a scene of a crime, that they were just really excited about something.

"Where did you get so many pretty dolls? Can I have them in my room? I really love this one. Isn't she the most beautiful baby you ever saw in your entire life? I bet I have some clothes that will fit her. Can I have her, Mom? Can I have her, please?"

Destiny pulled out one of the dining room chairs and sat. She looked from her daughter to the mess of ugly dolls on the table. "You really want to keep all of these dolls? Are you sure? You already have a room full of toys as it is."

Destiny finally focused on the doll that Krissy was waving about in the air. "Where did you find her? I don't remember unpacking her."

Krissy must have thought Destiny was going to take the doll away from her, because she pulled it into a tight hug up against her chest. "I can have her? She was on my bed. I thought you wanted me to have her."

If Destiny wasn't already confused enough, that statement made her try and think over everything she had done that weekend, but no matter how hard she tried she couldn't remember ever taking any of the dolls into her daughter's room. The fact was she had not gone into Krissy's room at all, because she had known that given the opportunity, Sassy would have slipped through the opened door and wouldn't have come out again unless dragged out. Destiny had purposely closed the bedroom door Friday night and hadn't opened it since, so how had the doll gotten onto Krissy's bed?

Destiny shook her head to try and clear up her thoughts. She was surely losing her mind. Between the divorce and her mother's death, she hadn't had a rational thought in months. Accepting the fact that she had to be the one who put the doll on Krissy's bed meant she had to have unpacked the doll, thought it was cute enough that Krissy would like to have it, and then that rationally meant she had to have put it on her daughter's bed. Lord, she needed a vacation away from the stress and drama. Maybe she could take a couple of weeks off from work and she and Krissy could rent a condo on the beach somewhere. That sounded absolutely heavenly.

"Can I have her, Mom?"

Regina Puckett

Destiny focused again on Krissy and realized she had been sitting there for some time without answering. She stood and smiled. "Of course. I don't think you need all of these dolls though. Let me first finish unpacking them and we'll go through them together to see which ones you really want to keep and which ones we can give away."

Krissy ran over and hugged her, and then turned to leave the room. It was only then Destiny realized Sassy was nowhere to be seen. That was unusual, since wherever Krissy was, the dog was always close by. "Where's Sassy?"

Krissy only stopped long enough to shrug. She called back over her shoulder. "She ran out of the bedroom when she saw my baby doll on the bed."

Destiny followed Krissy out of the room and went in search of Sassy. She thought that maybe the dog had hidden in her bedroom since that was where she had been since Krissy had left with Tony on Friday. She searched her room first. Not finding the terrier there, Destiny went from room to room calling Sassy's name, looking behind and under furniture, and even behind all of the curtains. She finally heard whining and followed the sound to the back door. When she opened it, Sassy was sitting there staring up and whining, as if she had been put in time out and was hoping against hope that all had been forgiven.

"How did you get out here? Did Krissy let you out?" Of course, Sassy didn't answer but went running between Destiny's legs into the house. By the time Destiny had closed the door and turned around, the dog had disappeared. Destiny headed back to Krissy's room. She found Sassy sitting outside the closed door staring and whining for someone to let her inside. Destiny opened the door and Sassy ran in but stopped dead in her tracks when she saw Krissy sitting in the middle of the bed, brushing the new doll's hair.

Sassy sniffed the air and began howling. Krissy dropped the doll and covered her ears.

"Mom. Make her stop!"

Not knowing which one was making the most noise but determined to bring to an end some of it, Destiny picked up the dog. The moment she did Sassy stopped howling and buried her face in the crook of her arm. The small terrier was

Regina Puckett

trembling, but she continued to express her displeasure by letting out a low rumbling sound that verged on becoming a growl at any moment. "What is wrong with you? Are you jealous of a doll? You've never acted like this before."

Destiny tucked the small terrier under her arm and looked over at Krissy. I'll lock her in my bathroom for a little while. I think you being away from so long must have upset her more than I thought. Maybe she can get a short nap and all will be better in an hour or two."

She glanced over at the clothes hanging out of her daughter's dresser drawers. The room had been spotless before Krissy's return home. "Stop playing long enough to straighten this room up. I'll have dinner ready in about thirty minutes. Clean your room, wash your hands and face and I'll holler for you when the food is on the table."

Destiny headed out but stopped at the door and turned. "I'm happy to see you, Baby. I sure have missed you. Did you have fun this weekend with your dad?"

Krissy bunched her face into a comical knot while she thought over the question. "Daddy kept kissing Beverly. Every time I came into the room, he yelled for me to get back into my room. I don't like Beverly. She kept taking her blouse off. Why did she keep taking her blouse off for, Mommy?"

Destiny had no idea how to answer this question. "Maybe she was hot."

Krissy nodded and looked thoughtful for a minute. "That's what Daddy said. I thought he must be teasing though, because all weekend long Beverly kept complaining about how low Daddy had the air set. She made him rub her feet because they were cold."

Okay. There was a much needed talk coming about what was appropriate to do when Krissy was at Tony's house and what wasn't. The man obviously had no clue how to keep his jeans zipped. She sighed. "Maybe her chest was hot but her feet were cold."

Krissy giggled. "You're silly, Mommy."

Destiny smiled but pointed toward the clothes hanging out of the dresser drawers. "I know, but don't forget to clean your mess up. Dinner is in a few minutes." She closed the door, but could still clearly hear Krissy talking to her doll. It was so good to have her back in the house.

She pulled the dog around so they were eye to eye. "No howling or growling in the house. You're going to have to learn to share Krissy."

Sassy whined.

"I know. I don't much like it either, but it's a fact of life. Learn to cope like everyone else."

Destiny carried Sassy into her bathroom, laid her on the nearest rug, and closed the door so she couldn't get out. The next couple of hours passed in a happy blur of eating, chatter, and bathing. Krissy begged to stay up thirty more minutes to watch one of her shows, claiming that she would just die if she didn't see it. The two them released Sassy from her confinement in the bathroom and the three of them snuggled up on the couch together to watch the show.

Sassy took her normal place across Krissy's legs. No matter if the two of them were on the couch or on Krissy's bed for the night, that was Sassy's self-appointed spot. Destiny believed the small dog thought she was Krissy's guardian and no one could get to her friend if that was where she was stationed.

Looking over at the two of them, Destiny had to smile with contentment. Now it felt like home again. She didn't understand what had gotten into the dog earlier, but all seemed to be right with the world again. About halfway into the show, Krissy's eyes began to droop. The next time Destiny glanced down, Krissy had leaned completely against her and was fast asleep. Sassy was sound asleep too, but while Destiny didn't wake her daughter, she did nudge the dog awake so she could follow them back to the bedroom. There was no way Destiny was going to try and carry both of them.

Destiny tucked Krissy under the covers, kissed the end of her nose, and stood back while Sassy jumped onto the bed and laid across Krissy's legs. Destiny bent and picked up the doll off of the floor and was going to tuck it under the covers with Krissy, but the minute she made toward the bed, Sassy's head popped up and growled. It was just a low warning growl but it sent shivers down Destiny's spine. She stopped in her tracks, stood there for a moment, and assessed the situation.

She finally shook her head, carried the doll

over to the dresser, and set it there alongside Krissy's small jewelry box and moons-and-stars nightlight. On her way out of the room, she stopped and whispered to Sassy. "Don't get used to me giving in to you every time. You're going to have to get used to sharing. I'm giving you fair warning."

Sassy snuggled her chin between her paws and sighed. Destiny grinned and left the room. She was pretty sure she had just been played, but she was much too tired to press the point. She wasn't certain why she was arguing with a dog anyway. She must have gotten used to the daily rows with Tony. Now she was just making things up to fight about.

She turned the covers to her own bed down and slid under them. She fell asleep almost as soon as her head hit the pillow. It didn't feel as if she had been in bed very long, when a sound woke her up. She glanced over at the clock radio and it read a little after midnight. She turned onto her other side and snuggled under the covers deeper, thinking that she must have been hearing things. She had just gotten comfortable, when she heard whispering. Thinking that Sassy had disturbed Krissy because she needed to go outside, Destiny got up and headed toward Krissy's room. She stopped in her own bedroom doorway though, and looked at Krissy's closed door. She never closed her door because she wanted to be able to hear Krissy if she ever called out and needed anything. Since she had just woken up and her brain cells weren't snapping and burning like they should have been, she decided that she must have closed it without thinking when she had left her daughter's room earlier.

Assuming that was the answer, Destiny grabbed the handle, turned it, and quietly opened the door. For a moment, she stopped in her tracks upon entering the room, because for a brief moment there appeared to be a shadow on the wall that looked as if someone was bending over the bed, hovering over Krissy. But, the longer she stared, the less it appeared to be a person and more like large shadows casted from the moving moons-and-stars lampshade on Krissy's nightlight. Even after reaching that conclusion, it took a moment for Destiny's heart to stop hammering against her eardrums.

She stood just inside of Krissy's room and tried to determine what it was about the room that was still bothering her. It took her a moment to realize that Sassy wasn't lying across Krissy's legs any longer, and the doll was now tucked under the covers with Krissy. Had Krissy woken up and realized the doll wasn't with her? That was it. Of course, that was it. But where was Sassy? Destiny turned and left Krissy's room and went in search of the terrier.

She searched each and every room again, just as she had earlier, but the dog was nowhere to be found. Going on a hunch, she went to the back door and opened it. There was Sassy shivering on the doormat. She whined as soon as she saw Destiny, came over, and sniffed her ankles. After sniffing for a long time, she finally licked one of them and then sat on Destiny's foot. Destiny shut and locked the door again before picking up Sassy and cradling her in the crook of her arm.

"What is going on? Did Krissy put you outside? I thought she was too afraid of the dark to go through house without me."

She pulled Sassy up so they were eye to eye. "Did you have to go potty? You should have come and gotten me up. You know Krissy isn't supposed to unlock these doors at night. What if there had been a prowler out here? You could have gotten both of you hurt, killed, or worse."

After the stern lecture, Sassy licked the end of Destiny's nose and whimpered. Destiny tugged the terrier in close to her breast and sighed. "There's no point in trying to sweet talk me now. I have to get up early to take Krissy to school before I go to work. If I have to get up again, you're going to be in big trouble."

Sassy sighed and laid her chin on the swell of Destiny's breast. "We'll talk about this tomorrow. Krissy has some explaining to do herself."

Destiny headed back to Krissy's room with the full intention of putting Sassy back onto Krissy's bed, but Destiny stopped short when she saw Krissy's door was closed again. Sassy's head popped up and she began to growl. "Hush. If you wake up Krissy, you're going to be in big trouble. Since it doesn't look like you're going to behave, I'm going to put you back in my bathroom. I'll let you out in the morning, but I can't take any chance you might wake up Krissy right now."

Destiny carried Sassy to her bathroom, put

Regina Puckett

her onto the floor and shut the door. She then walked back her daughter's room and opened the door. When she first opened the door, it sounded as if there was someone in the bed whispering, so she carefully tiptoed over and looked at Krissy. She certainly had all of the appearances of being sound asleep. Her little mouth was partially open and her face had that peaceful expression of a child who was dead to the world. Destiny looked at her for a moment before deciding she had imagined the shadow on the wall, the closed door, and the whispering. There was no doubt there was nothing wrong in the room or with her daughter. It was time just to go back to bed and back to sleep.

It didn't take but a few moments to slip back into a deep sleep. The next morning she showered and dressed before letting Sassy out to do her business in the backyard, and it was only then she went in to wake Krissy. The door was closed again. There was no explanation for it, so she didn't even bother thinking about it again. She was running a few minutes behind, so she just opened it and entered the darkened room. With the blinds and thick curtains, there was no sunlight to brighten the room. For some reason, the nightlight was no longer lit. She reached over and flipped the light switch. The moment the overhead light came on, she could see that Krissy wasn't in the bed or the room.

"Krissy?" She crossed the hallway to her room, but after a quick search of the bedroom and bathroom, she soon discovered that Krissy wasn't in those rooms either. Destiny headed into the kitchen. Maybe somewhere along the way, their paths crossed without them realizing it. It didn't take long to see that Krissy wasn't in there, so Destiny checked the living room and then the dining room. The only things in the dining room were the spooky clown and all of his girlfriends. The clown's mouth popped open and then snapped closed again as if to let her know he was still in charge of the dining room and all of its inmates.

"Oh shut up."

His malevolent grin was freaky even in broad daylight so she looked away from Creepy Clown Guy. "Krissy! We're running behind, hon. Let's eat and get dressed. I can't afford to be late again."

Regina Puckett

Nothing but silence answered. She stood in the middle of the dining room, dumbfounded. Second by second, the earlier horrible feeling that something was wrong was quickly turning into a full blown panic. "Don't be stupid. She's here."

She heard Sassy yapping outside. "Of course. She went outside to play with Sassy. You are really beginning to become just like your mother. You're overreacting to everything these days."

Convincing herself that everything was going to be just fine, Destiny slowly forced the panic to seep out of her body. Destiny headed back into the kitchen and opened the backdoor. Sassy ran in and through the kitchen in the direction of the bedrooms. She barked continuously.

Destiny shook her head at the noise but continued out into the backyard. "Krissy? Come on, hon. We have to eat and get out of here. You're going to be late for school and I'm going to be late to work."

She crossed the patio, stepped off into the grass, and looked around. Krissy was nowhere to be seen. "Krissy? Are you out here?" No one answered back. Total panic took over when Destiny realized Krissy wasn't outside either. She ran back into the house. She didn't even bother to shut the door behind her but took off in a run throughout the house calling her daughter's name the entire time.

Destiny wound up in Krissy's room again only finding Sassy in the middle of Krissy's bed. The terrier was lying across the legs of an unfamiliar doll.

"Where's Krissy? Where's she at? Where's she at? Where's she at?" She sat on the edge of the bed and leaned forward. She cupped her face between her palms and focused on breathing in and out. She finally stood and wiped the hair that was now hanging down in her eyes, as if that would be enough to clear away the cobwebs.

"I have to call the police. They'll be able to find her."

Sassy popped her head up off of her paws when Destiny stood, but the terrier didn't budge from safe guarding the doll.

Destiny dashed across the hall to use the nearest phone. While it seemed as if it took the police an extraordinarily long time to come to the house, in reality it only took a few minutes. The house and yard soon filled with cars and officers. She tried to explain everything that had taken place the night before and that morning. She wasn't certain how any of it could be of any use to the police, since she had not heard anything else after she returned to bed. They wanted to know if she had relocked the door after letting the dog in, or if she thought Krissy might have gotten up searching for Sassy and might have gone outside.

Destiny was almost positive she had locked the door after letting Sassy in, and she was fairly certain Krissy would never venture outside on her own. The truth was, she was now unsure about everything that had happened the night before. Destiny never would have thought that Krissy would have let Sassy out by herself in the first place, so how could she be certain whether or not her daughter would have been brave enough to venture out into the dark backyard to go search for Sassy? None of it made any sense. What if she had left the door unlocked and someone came in and took Krissy? Wouldn't she have heard that? Wouldn't her daughter have cried out or called for her? There was no way a stranger would have been able to enter the house without Sassy barking like crazy and waking her up.

Destiny tried not to fall apart throughout all of the questioning. What she really wanted to do was to get up and go outside to begin looking for Krissy herself. What if the officers weren't taking it seriously enough and weren't going door to door to make certain one of the neighbors hadn't stolen her daughter? There were too many what ifs and no answers. Her head felt as if it was going to explode. Every time the door opened, she looked at it, hoping someone was going to come in at any moment with Krissy in their arms saying they had found her sitting on the curb or something. Where was she?

Just when Destiny didn't think it could get any worse, Tony came bounding through the door shouting to anyone within listening distance he wanted to know what was going on and what had the bitch done with his daughter. Several officers ushered him to another room, and while every now and then she could hear Tony's raised voice, she couldn't hear what they were saying. Someone finally bought her a hot cup of coffee and while the thought of drinking anything made her want to throw up it was good to hold onto something.

Regina Puckett

Somewhere around lunch time, a neighbor came in with a plate of sandwiches and tried to talk her into eating something, but there was no way she was going to be able to swallow anything without gagging. Finally, to have a moment alone she got up and headed back to Krissy's room. She saw Tony and several of the officers huddled together in the dining room, whispering. Everyone stopped as she passed through. She could feel their stares even though she could no longer see them. It made her feel a little uneasy but she had too many other worries to be too concerned over what they were discussing among themselves.

When she entered Krissy's room, she found Sassy still lying in the same spot on the bed with her body in a protective stance across the doll's legs. She sat on the edge of the bed and stared at Krissy's dresser not really focusing on anything. It took a moment to figure out what was bothering her about the room. It struck her like a bolt of lightning that all of the dresser drawers had been pulled out again and several of Krissy's clothes were hanging half in and half out. The cord to the nightlight was out of the outlet and it was hanging loose in the front of the dresser.

Had the police searched her daughter's

room looking for evidence? That made sense. They would want to know everything about the situation. She finally glanced over at Sassy and at once, the dog picked her head up from the bed.

"Do you need to go outside? You haven't gone outside since early this morning."

She stood and made a motion for Sassy to follow her. "Come on, girl. Let's get some fresh air. Krissy isn't here. There's no point in you making yourself sick waiting in here for her. You can protect our little girl when she gets back. Okay?"

Sassy positioned her head squarely back in between her paws and didn't budge from her spot.

"Come, Sassy. Let's go."

Sassy whined but didn't move.

Destiny sat and reached over and pulled the doll out from under Sassy. The terrier ran over and began yelping as if trying to tell Destiny something.

Destiny absentmindedly patted the dog's head while examining the doll. Something about it was worrisome, but she was either too tired or worried to be able to put a finger on the exact cause of her concern.

She was still holding the doll when Tony came in. "Why don't you just tell everyone where Krissy is at? Don't you think this has gone on for far too long? I know you hate me, but you don't have to hurt my daughter to get back at me."

Destiny turned the doll around and sat it in her lap as she would have a child. She hugged it up against her stomach and chest for a sense of some type of comfort.

Nothing Tony said made any sense. "What are you talking about? Why is everything always about you, Tony? Your daughter is out there somewhere. She's alone, she's lost, and someone could be at the very moment hurting her and all you can think about is yourself."

They stared at each other for a long time before Tony shifted his gaze downward and onto the doll in Destiny's lap. "When did you get her?"

Destiny looked at the top of the doll's head. "It was one of Mom's. I was unpacking them yesterday when you bought Krissy home. I guess she saw it and bought it back here."

Regina Puckett

"Your mom must have bought it because it looks so much like Krissy."

He moved further into the room and stood in front of her while she examined the doll closer. He made a movement as if he was going to take it away from her, but she waved him off. Everything about the doll looked like Krissy; the short, blonde curly hair, the big blue eyes, and even her clothes were the mirror imagine of Krissy's bedclothes. Where had Krissy found this doll?

"I don't know when she found it. It's not one of the ones I already unpacked yesterday."

The more she looked, the harder her heart beat. She knew that if she told Tony that the doll had on the same pajamas and socks Krissy had been wearing to bed the night before, he wouldn't believe her. She stood and laid the doll back onto the bed so she could look around Krissy's room. She had been too busy looking for Krissy earlier really to look at anything.

The moment she put the doll back onto the bed, Sassy laid her body across its legs. When the terrier had done that earlier, Destiny hadn't thought anything about it, but this time it sent a shiver down her spine.

"What are you doing?"

Destiny didn't bother answering. Where was the doll Krissy had been sleeping with the night before? She looked through all of the dresser drawers, and when she didn't find the doll there, she moved over to the bed and searched through the covers and then underneath the bed. Not finding the doll there, she moved onto the closet.

Tony followed her every step of the way. "What are you searching for? If you tell me, maybe I can help."

Destiny stopped long enough to glance his way. "I'm looking for the doll she brought in here last night."

He pointed toward the bed. "You were just holding a doll. Isn't that it?"

She shook her head and dove into the mess Krissy called a closet. There were clothes, shoes, and boxes of games in just about ever of it but no dolls.

"For crying out loud! Tell me what this doll

looks like, and I'll help."

She fluttered her hands in the air but no words came out. She finally screeched out. "It's a doll! I don't know! It's nothing special. It's just a damn doll."

She brushed by him with the intention of searching the other side of the bed but stopped short. Leaning against the wall on the other side of the bed was the clown that had freaked her out the night before. It was just the last straw, so she sat on the foot of the bed and stared over at the clown. There was no way the police had carried it in here. It had been in the dining room this morning. That much she was certain about.

She felt Tony staring at her as if she had lost her mind, but she didn't care. Too many things didn't make sense. No. None of it made any sense. Where was the doll her daughter had brought into the room the night before, when had the clown doll been brought in, where had the doll that Sassy was guarding come from, but the most important question was where had her daughter disappeared to?

She looked behind her at Sassy and the

doll on which he was lying across. Sassy looked back and whined. "What are you trying to tell me? You're not guarding Krissy. That isn't Krissy. I know that isn't Krissy." She could hear her voice getting louder and louder, but she no longer had the ability to control the panic or confusion.

No rational person would even consider such a thing. Maybe this was a trick. Had Tony planned this to drive her crazy? She shook that thought out of her head and placed her face into the palms of her hands. She leaned forward with her elbows propped on the edge of her knees. *Think. Think about what you know.*

Krissy and I had supper. She helped me put the dishes in the dishwasher. I washed her hair and gave her a bath before cutting the television on for her to watch so I could take a shower. We both let Sassy out of the bathroom and settled onto the couch to watch Krissy's show together. Krissy fell asleep. I carried her to bed. I woke up and found Sassy outside. I put her in my bathroom so she wouldn't wake up Krissy with her whining. What am I missing? What did I do wrong? Did I leave the kitchen door unlocked when I let Sassy in? Did I leave it unlocked and a stranger came in and took my baby away?

Regina Puckett

She sat up, reached over, and pulled the doll out from under Sassy. She could see out of the corner of her eye that Tony had slipped out of the bedroom. It didn't matter. She had to figure out what was going on. She examined every inch of the doll again. As soon as she was finished examining the doll again, she hugged it up against her chest and rocked back and forth. She was no longer able to think about anything, but that *it couldn't be*. There was no way this doll was her daughter, but she had on the same pajamas, socks and even right down to the same exact underpants. She rocked and rocked but stopped when she realized her blouse was wet. Destiny pulled the doll away from her body, looked at the wet spot in the middle of her blouse, and then looked back at the doll's face. There was a steady stream of tears running down from the corners of both of the doll's eyes.

Destiny let out a loud wail and then clutched the doll back to her chest. Just then, several officers ran into the room to see what was taking place.

The officer in charge finally walked up to her. "We need to talk."

Destiny drew in a long breath before

looking at him. "What?"

His face no longer had any of the earlier signs of compassion or concern on it, but now in their place was a steely stare and a firmly set jaw. "I'm driving you to the station where we can talk."

Confusion on top of confusion. The entire world had gone insane sometime between yesterday and this morning. "I'm staying here. What if Krissy shows up while I'm gone? We can talk here."

"I'll leave an officer here in case that happens, but we both know that isn't going to happen. Don't we?"

Destiny ran her hand through her hair and stared at the officer. "What are you trying to say? Do you know something I don't know? Is my daughter dead? Have you found her body and you're not telling me?"

She wanted to pound on his chest just to stop him from staring at her as if he knew something she didn't know. Krissy was her daughter. If someone knew something, they needed to tell her. She continued holding onto the doll and tried not to look down at the wet spot on her blouse growing wetter by the moment. No one else seemed to notice so maybe it was just her imagination going crazy from worrying so much about Krissy. Her daughter wasn't in her arms crying because she was stuck inside of a doll's body and couldn't get out. The tears weren't real. None of this was real. Any moment now, she was going to wake up from this nightmare and her daughter was going to be tucked safely in her own bed. These officers weren't going to be in her house staring at her as if she had committed some type of crime.

She closed her eyes again and began to rock the doll in her arms. She tried shutting out the other noises in the room and concentrated on waking up. Any minute, it was all going to go away. She jerked back to reality when the officer yanked the doll out of her arms and tossed it onto the bed. He then gripped her arm with the intention of pulling her out of the room, but the moment he touched her Sassy jumped through the air, like an attack dog, and went for the officer's throat.

What happened next went by in such a blur that Destiny wasn't certain how it ended so badly. She saw Sassy's attack but looked away when all of the other officers came rushing into

Regina Puckett

the room. One officer shoved her backward and forced her backwards onto the bed and for some unknown reason, another officer fell on top of her. There was the sound of heavy breathing, men cussing, one man screaming in pain and then the sound of a gun being discharged. When the officer was finally able to stand again, she sat up, but soon wished she had stayed hidden amongst the bedcovers. There was blood splattered everywhere and Sassy was lying lifelessly against the end of the foot of the bed.

Destiny had no more absorbed all of that before the officer who had been attacked roughly yanked her up from the bed and pulled her out of the room. She tried getting out of his grasp long enough to run back and get the doll from off of the bed. The dog attack had only made the officer angrier, so his response to her trying to go back into the room was to pull her as hard as he could up against his chest. For the first time since Sassy attacked him, she saw the jagged gash on the side of his neck and the blood that was now freely flowing from the open wound.

"If I were you, I wouldn't do anything else to try my patience. You might have a little accident before we reach the station. You understand what

Regina Puckett

I'm trying to say to you?"

She stared into the deep recesses of his dilated black pupils. "I need to take the doll with me." She thought for a moment he was going to strike her but his training must have regained control over the surge of pain and adrenaline. Instead of hitting her, as she could clearly see he had thought about, he raised and lowered in his hand again in the span of seconds.

He pulled her out of the room. "No."

She pulled and screamed, and tried everything within her power to get out of his tight grip, but she couldn't break free. They passed Tony as they left the house. He followed them out onto the porch and watched gleefully as the angry officer shoved her into the back of the patrol car. Tony smiled and waved as the police car pulled out of the driveway.

Nothing she said at the station could convince them she hadn't harmed Krissy to get even with Tony. She tried telling them that she had wanted the divorce and not Tony. However, while she had been in the living room praying for her daughter to be found and retuned back home

Regina Puckett

safely, Tony had been in the dining room with the police telling them all sorts of lies about how she had threatened to kill him and Krissy and then kill herself if he didn't come back to her. He had told them about bringing his girlfriend along when he had brought Krissy back to the house the night before. He was able to convince them that the reason she had harmed their daughter was that she had finally figured out that he had moved on with his life and that he was never going go back to her.

For some unknown reason, the police had believed every hateful, made-up lie. They thought she had killed Krissy and taken her body off and hidden it sometime during the night before calling them with the fabricated story that Krissy was missing. Destiny couldn't say or do anything to convince them otherwise. The police leaned toward believing Tony's made up lies, because just weeks before another woman in the state had done just the exact thing they were now accusing her of doing. It looked bad, but she didn't care. She was too confused and scared to know what to think or believe.

Destiny walked around the interrogation room for about the hundredth time, trying to think what she could do to fix this. Was her daughter really a doll? How could that be? It couldn't. It just didn't make any sense. She walked in circles for hours, praying and hoping the police would finally see reason and let her go. She had to get home before Krissy did. Her daughter had to be so frightened. When Destiny was finally was too exhausted to walk any longer, she sat in one of the straight back chairs and laid her head onto her arms on the wooden tabletop. Before she knew it, the night had turned to daylight again and she could hear the door handle rattling as someone held it to shove in a key to unlock it.

She sat back and wiped the sleep from her eyes, as the officer who had interrogated her for half of the night, came in and closed the door. He threw a file onto the table and stared at her. She was too tired to ask him anything, so she waited. He finally shifted his eyes from hers and leaned forward with his elbows braced onto his legs and knees. She watched him as he seemed to consider something. He finally sat back and ran both hands through his hair before turning back in her direction.

"Lady, I'm not certain what you're mixed up in, but this is the weirdest, most screwed up case I have ever been involved with."

Every fiber of her being ached to hear some good news about her daughter, but she waited because nothing about his expression said he had anything good to say.

"Are you hooked up with the occult or something? Because some bad shit went down last night. That's the only explanation I can come up with is, that has to do with some type of Satanic worship or something worse."

He opened the file to show a picture in the folder. Against her better judgment, Destiny looked down at it. She was relieved to see it wasn't of her daughter. The photo was of Tony and the young lady he had with him on Sunday when he took Krissy home. She leaned forward to get a better look at the photo because nothing about it made any sense. She finally looked back up at the officer and waited for him to explain it to her.

That seemed to make him angrier, because he slapped his palm against the photo and leaned forward in order to be face to face with her. "They're dead. They're both dead. I don't know how yet, but they looked scared to death. I got a call this morning from his cleaning lady and this is how she found them, clutching the bedcovers with their mouths opened as if they had died screaming." He pushed the photo her way and then shoved the back of her head so she was forced to lean forward to look at the photo whether she wanted to or not.

"Look at it. They're covered up with every one of those damn dolls from your house and off of your dining room table." He stabbed a fingertip directly on the doll sitting between Tony and his girlfriend.

"That's the clown from your daughter's room. I couldn't believe it at first, so I drove over to your townhouse and every last one of those dolls of yours were missing. All but one, that is. Someone took that one to your backyard. They put it in your trash barrel and set it on fire. I don't which one it was, because by the time we got there it was just a mass of charred plastic. I suspect it's the one you were trying to go back and get yesterday, because we couldn't find it at your husband's house.

Nothing up to that point had bothered Destiny; not seeing the frozen scream on Tony's face or the clown sitting between him and his dead girlfriend, but when the officer talked off-handedly about the burned doll in her waste barrel, she jumped up so fast her chair went flying back across the room. The officer was too surprised by her sudden reaction to do anything but sit and look at her fallen chair. While he sat there with his mouth hanging open, she launched herself across the table and began choking him. As soon as he regained use of his brain again, he pulled her hands away from his neck. She broke free and began scratching and clawing at his face and arms.

If she could have killed him with her bare hands she would have, but the room was soon filled to capacity with officers. It took almost of them and several attempts, but they finally pulled her off of him. They then threw her to the floor, and someone sat on top of her with his knee pressed painfully between her shoulder blades. They finally handcuffed her and began pulling her out of the room. She turned around as far she could and spat across the room at the officer that she had attacked.

She screamed at the top of her lungs. "He killed her! You brought me here and let him kill her! You, bastards, let him kill my daughter!" she screamed out to anyone who would listen. No one understood that it was their fault that Tony had the time and opportunity to burn his own daughter to death, but thank God for the dolls. They had taken care of him and his bitch. Just let her get out of the handcuffs into which they had locked her. The moment she was free, she was going to kill every last man and woman in the station for letting Tony kill her daughter!

George walked away from the scene being played out, as the officers carried Destiny down the hallway toward the area in the back where the cells were located. After she was out of sight, he turned back toward his partner. "You okay, Jeff?"

Jeff wiped at the blood running down his face. "I guess I'm just about as alright as I'm going to get, with still not knowing if that little girl is alive or dead yet."

George sat in one of the straight back chairs, leaned sideways, and propped an elbow onto the table's top. He let out a long weary sigh. "We took the cadaver dogs out to the house earlier this morning. They didn't find any indication of a dead body in the house but the dogs went crazy around that old burning barrel in the backyard."

"You don't think she burned that poor baby alive in that barrel do you? God help us all. What has this world come to? Every day I wake up and I have no idea what we are going to have to investigate next. Mothers and fathers are out there, as we speak, killing their children just to get back at each other. Aren't they the ones who are supposed to be protecting them from this big bad world of us? I sometimes think we're safer in the company of strangers than we are when we're with our own families."

Both men looked at each for a moment not saying anything, because what was there to say?

Finally, Jeff rubbed his forehead and grimaced. "Come on. We aren't solving anything back here. I need to go to my desk and take a couple of aspirins before we head back out to the scene."

George followed Jeff to his desk but collided into his back when Jeff stopped up short.

"Who the hell put the damn clown on my desk!"

Regina Puckett

WILL WORK FOR FOOD

Regina Puckett

"Sir!"

Doris tucked the purse a little more securely under her arm before tugging on Gerald's sleeve. It took several tries before her husband finally stopped pushing the food cart and turned to see what she wanted.

"What?" His voice came out as a strange mixture of irritation and forced patience, but his facial expression really gave away the fact that his sights had been firmly focused on getting to the car and that he hated the interruption.

After so many years of marriage, Doris was used to how moody shopping made him, so his abrupt tone didn't bother her in the least. "I think someone is trying to get your attention." She turned to see if the man, who had been on their heels since exiting the large food chain, was still following them.

Regina Puckett

Not only was he still there, but he had used the fact that they had stopped to his advantage. As soon as he had their full attention, the dirty man bowed his head and jammed both hands into the pockets of his filthy jeans. "I hate to be a bother, but could you spare me a few dollars? My car ran out of gas a few miles back. I'm trying to get home to my sick wife."

Gerald frowned before pointing toward the basket of food. "We are on a fixed income. What you see here is the last of this month's check. I can't help you. Sorry." Without so much as a backward glance, Gerald began pushing the basket again but this time at a faster pace.

Doris smiled with the hope that the beggar would understand just how sorry she was for not being able to help him, but instead of returning the smile with one of his own, he turned and spit onto the sidewalk. Without another word, he headed back to accost a young couple with a baby coming out of the store.

She glanced down at the disgusting glob of spit. "Well! That wasn't very nice."

She watched the couple stop to talk to the

beggar before she took off after Gerald. She was winded and overheated the time she reached the car.

Gerald didn't even bother looking up, but continued tossing the bags of groceries into the trunk. After the basket was finally empty of grocery bags, he turned and glared. "You know better than to encourage those kinds of people. Beggars are everywhere these days."

He waved his arm in a long loop around the parking lot. "There are at least a dozen of them just waiting for you to stop long enough so they can begin telling their sad tale about why they need money. Their wives or children are ill. Their cars are broken down or out of gas. I know how kindhearted you are, but let's face it; we can't help all of them. I bet most of them are lying anyway. My car would be out of gas too if I used every cent I had to buy booze or drugs. You need to grow up, Doris. These beggars want what we have had to work our entire lives for instead of the lot of them actually going out there and getting a job to earn the money for themselves. You show me a man who willing to work and that will be the man I'm willing to help."

Regina Puckett

As soon as Gerald finished his long speech, he pushed the cart over to the rack to leave with the others. After getting into the car he reached over and took Doris' hand. He had time to calm down so his voice now held a gentler tone. "I really do wish I could do more but we only have thirty dollars to last us for the next three weeks. What would happen if one of us needed to go to the doctor or something? Our social security checks just don't go as far as they need to. We can't save the world."

Doris listened to his lecture and blinked back tears. "I know you're right, but it's so hard telling people you can't help them."

Gerald didn't have anything to say to that, but just shook his head and started the car. He drove directly from the food store into the nearest gas station.

Doris stayed in the car while he went around to her side of the car to begin pumping gas. She was absentmindedly watching him, when she noticed from the side view mirror that a man was approaching the car. Gerald was too busy taking off the gas cap to notice the man's sudden appearance. The guy startled him when he tapped

Regina Puckett

him on the shoulder. She couldn't hear the words being exchanged but even before Gerald had the time to put in a couple of gallons of gas he removed the nozzle and quickly screwed the cap back on. He left the other man standing by the gas pump while he climbed back into the car.

"What happened?"

He locked the doors and then wiped off a layer of sweat from his upper lip before answering. "It was someone else asking for money. I tried explaining that I was charging the gas to my credit card but he didn't seem to believe that I couldn't afford to help him out. It's getting too dangerous to even stop for gas in broad daylight. Pretty soon these people are going to stop asking and just begin taking. That guy was pretty angry. I thought he was going to hit me."

He pulled out of the gas station and into traffic. "I'll stop at a gas station closer to home and finish filling up there."

Doris didn't say anything for a little while but watched the landscape go by without really seeing it. She finally turned slightly in Gerald's direction. "Maybe next month we can cut back on our expenses enough to have a few dollars with us every time we go out. I hate that we're never able to do anything to help. It just feels wrong to always have to tell these people 'no.'"

Gerald patted her knee. "You're too goodhearted. Even if we could afford to cut back, it's still impossible to help everyone. There are just too many people out there in need."

They drove in silence for a few minutes until Doris gasped. She reached over and tapped Gerald's arm. "Oh, Hon. Look at that. He has a little boy with him. I wonder how long they have been sitting out there in this heat?"

They were stopped about five car lengths for a red light at a busy intersection. Up by the corner, a grubby man who appeared to be about in his early thirties sat with a child who seemed to be about eight or nine years old. The man was clutching a cardboard sign that read, "Will work for food."

Doris stared at the two of them for a moment before looking back at her husband. "We have to help them. I know we don't have much money, but we do have food."

Gerald sighed. "What are you suggesting?"

For the first time all morning Doris felt a glimmer of hope. "Our grass needs cutting. It has been too hot for you to do it. We could offer to let that man cut the grass, and for payment, I'll cook a nice meal for them to eat and enough food to pack so they can take some of it with them for later."

She tried to not sound too whiney but she really wanted to help that little boy. Their oldest grandson was about the same age. "We could do that, couldn't we?"

Gerald shook his head and rolled his eyes in resignation. But he did flip the turn signal on so he could pull the car off onto the shoulder and out of traffic. As soon as the car was parked, he got out without another word, but a couple of minutes later, he came back with the man and young boy following close behind.

It was only after everyone was settled that Doris turned in her seat. The sight of the boy and man up close was even more heart shattering than from afar. Both of them were bright red from the heat, paper-thin, and they had a hopeless look of despair about them.

Regina Puckett

"I insist that the two of you drink my homemade sweet tea and eat a good meal before you start on the yard. There's plenty of daylight left..."

Before all of the words were out of her mouth the man was shaking his head. "No. We'll get the job done first. That's the work ethics I'm teaching my boy, Andy, here. You don't eat until you've earned it. I don't want him thinking that things in life are free. We may be poor, but we ain't no beggars. We ain't asking for no handouts. My old man taught me that a man earns his way in life. I want my son raised up the same way I was. It's a hard life but we got each other. As long as we got each other, and the strength the Good Lord gave us, we ain't never gonna want for nothing."

All that was said with abruptness, but the look of pride on his face toned down the harshness of it just a smidgen.

The fierce expression on his face might have been enough to create a little bit of doubt in the mind of a lesser woman, but Doris was made of sterner stuff and was fully determined to do her good deed. "At least have some tea before you begin working on the yard. I wouldn't want you to have a heatstroke because of dehydration." Doris was a kindhearted soul, but she could also be firm when she took a mind to be. She didn't give the man time to refuse but reached back and offered her hand. "I'm Doris Langford and this is my husband, Gerald."

Gerald took his eyes off of the road long enough to nod a greeting into the rearview mirror.

The young man returned the nod and then offered a grimy and calloused hand to Doris. "I'm Michael Benson, and this here is my son, Andy. My wife is back home sick. I'll accept your kind offer of that sweet tea, if you'll let me and the boy wrap that meal up and take it back home with us to share with my wife. We ain't had a good meal in eight days. I was able to kill a squirrel a couple of days back."

They were both so sickly looking Doris wasn't certain how they were going to survive through the heat of the day without a good meal under their belts, much less wait to eat until after returning home. It seemed really unfair to her that Michael was making his son wait for his food too, since the child already looked half starved to death.

"You are more than welcome to eat before you leave, and I'll wrap up more food for you to take home with you. Cutting the grass is worth more than one meal."

He held up a hand to forestall another word from her. "I teach my boy that no one eats until everyone eats. It's our way. I'm meaning no disrespect to you, but I couldn't eat knowing my wife was back home hungry. I know Andy couldn't either, so the faster we get the yard work finished, the faster we can all sit down together for a good meal."

Gerald must have sensed her urge to continue arguing, because he reached over and took her hand. They had been married long enough that she understood when he wanted her to stop arguing, so while so she struggled with Michael's logic the rest of the way home, she managed to keep her concerns to herself. By the time they pulled into the driveway, she reached the conclusion that everyone had their own beliefs and it wasn't her place to try and change their minds. All she could do now was to offer the food and it was up to them when they wanted to eat it.

When she headed into the house to cook,

Regina Puckett

Gerald took Michael and Andy out to his workshop to gas up the weed eater and lawnmower. She was in the middle of peeling potatoes when, from the kitchen window, she saw Andy pushing the lawnmower by. The handle of the mower was so tall that Andy's arms were raised up over his head. It looked like it was hard for him to push the large mower, but he bore a determined expression and seemed to be getting the job done.

As soon as Gerald came from outside and into the kitchen, she handed him the tea pitcher and two glasses. "At least go sit this out on the picnic table. Maybe Michael will let Andy drink something in a little while." She leaned her hip up against the cabinet and pointed her paring knife in her husband's direction. "What kind of father makes his son work when it's obvious how hungry the child is? There are ethics and then there's just plain stupidity."

Gerald shook his head. "Doris, it's not our place to fix everybody. We gave 'em work to do. The man has rules he lives by. At least he's not out there stealing and teaching his son to do the same thing. There are worse rules to have. You're going to have to learn to pick your battles. You wanted to help someone out today, and we have. Let's do this his way. Let him have his pride. Okay?"

Doris grunted her disapproval but knew better than to argue with Gerald when he thought he had a point. It would have been like arguing with a stone statue, so she went back to peeling potatoes. It was took a few minutes for him to take the tea and glasses out to the picnic table, and when he came back inside he stopped long enough to kiss her on the cheek.

The sound of the lawn mower and weed eater drowned out the television show Gerald was watching in the living room. Every now and then Doris would look outside to make certain Andy didn't need anything. Even though Michael didn't seem to be too concerned over the child's welfare, it did trouble her that Andy was having to work so hard out there in the August heat, but every time she peeked outside, Andy was still doggedly pushing that mower as if he was used to the hard work. But then for all she knew, he was used to working long hard hours with little or no food. While she wished there was more she could do for them, she could tell by how proud Michael appeared to be, that if they tried to do more than had already been agreed on, he would probably just refuse it.

Regina Puckett

Doris put Gerald's lunch onto the table but she didn't eat anything. She couldn't sit down to a meal knowing there was a boy outside working who hadn't eaten in days. While Gerald ate his lunch, she packed up the leftovers and then added several sacks of canned goods as payment for the lawn work. It seemed only fair for all of the hard work the father and son were outside doing.

When Gerald was finished eating, he brought his dishes over to the sink and put them there for her to wash. "I'm going to put the chainsaw in the trunk of the car. Michael asked if he could borrow it. He has a couple of trees that fell down in his yard during that last rain storm. They're just about finished out there. You get everything together that needs to go with us, and I'll come back to get it in just a minute."

Doris picked up the dirty dishes and put them into the hot dishwater. She turned to face Gerald. "Are you going to help him cut up those trees? It will speed things up and we can be home before it gets too dark. You know you don't see as well as you used to after dark."

"Yep. You know how peculiar I am about my chainsaw. The last person who borrowed it tore it up and it cost me almost a hundred dollars to have someone fix it. My daddy always told me that a man takes good care of his tools, because one day his tools will take good care of him."

Doris wiped a tear from the corner of her eye. "I miss your daddy. He knew how to take good care of his family. He taught all of his boys to be good providers. There's never been a day the kids or I have ever wanted for anything. There's always been plenty of food on the table and a roof over our heads."

Gerald nodded. "That's one of the reasons I hate just handing money over to these people out there begging on the street corners. A man should always be willing to work for his food."

He kissed her cheek. "That's was a really good lunch today. That meatloaf might have been the best you have ever cooked before."

"It's all in the spices."

The roaring of the lawnmower stopped. Gerald leaned across Doris to look out the kitchen window. "It looks like Andy and Michael are done with the yard work. The sooner we get them home the sooner they can eat. They sure have earned it."

He grabbed a couple of the bags Doris had packed earlier. "Be ready in fifteen minutes."

She nodded and hurriedly washed the rest of the dishes so she could gather up everything for Gerald to carry out to the car. She was ready and waiting by the time he returned for the rest of the bags.

On the way to take Michael and Andy home, Doris tried several times to begin a conversation, but Michael only answered the questions with one word sentences or with only a nod that she couldn't see from the front seat.

Finally, after giving up all hope of anyone having anything to talk about, Michael asked Gerald a question without being prompted. "Mr. Langford do you ever go hunting? We have some nice woods out our way with a lot of good game out there in it. Sometimes that's all we have to eat is what I can shoot."

Gerald glanced in the mirror before answering. "No. I can't say that I ever cared much for hunting."

There was more silence until Gerald finally spoke again. "My dad did teach me how to fish though. I enjoy a good fishing trip. You just sit there and let the fish do all of the work. That's the only other way I'll go looking for food besides the supermarket. I've always been a little afraid of guns. You get shot out in the woods and you could bleed to death before anyone ever found you."

That declaration shut all other conversation down.

The trip lasted about thirty more minutes and when they finally did arrive, the shock of seeing where Michael and Andy lived almost caused Doris to let out an involuntarily gasp, but fortunately she stopped herself just before it escaped. It would have been beyond rude to let them see just how horrified she was that anyone could possibly live in such primitive conditions. The Benson's house turned out to be no more than a crumbling shack. It was located about a mile down a dirt drive that was probably impossible to drive on when wet. If it had ever had any gravel on it, it was impossible to tell by the condition it was in now. Since there wasn't a car in sight, it probably didn't even matter. The house was so far from town, Doris had to wonder how Andy and Michael had gotten to town that morning. Either they had hitched a ride after reaching the highway or they had walked the entire ten miles into town.

There didn't appear to be another house in sight. The place was so far back into a densely wooded area that a house could have been close by and still not be seen. The place had an eerie silence that gave Doris the creeps. She considered staying in the car, but knew that would be rude, so she climbed out when everyone else did. She pretended not to notice how isolated from civilization the place was.

It was only after the four of them were out of the car that Michael finally spoke again. "Andy, help Mrs. Langford carry the food inside to your mom. Then you come back out to help me cut these trees into firewood so Mr. Langford can take his chainsaw back home when he leaves."

Doris opened her mouth to protest but at that moment, a huge, red dog came loping out to the car. It planted both paws in the middle of Michael's chest, but he swatted the dog away. "Get off of me and get back to the house."

Doris was surprised when the dog did exactly as it was told to do. The poor thing's ribs were clearly showing through its dull red hair. It

Regina Puckett

looked as if the entire family was starving to death together. Since it appeared as if Michael was determined to now cut the trees up into firewood before he was going to let anyone eat, she rushed to the rear of the car to get the food out. She dreaded to see what kind of shape the inside of the house was in, but it seemed to be a pointless act to put off going inside any longer. Andy joined her, so she handed him a couple of the lighter bags to carry while she pulled out the canned goods for herself to carry.

She followed Andy through the overgrown weeds in the yard and right on into the house. Once inside, she was pleasantly surprised by how clean the place was. All of the furniture appeared to be odds and ends that they had either gotten from the dump or hand me downs. But as shabby as everything was, there didn't appear to be a speck of dust anywhere.

For the first time since picking up the two from the side of the road Andy spoke. "Mom!"

Doris was so surprised by the sound of his voice she almost dropped the sacks she was carrying. Fortunately she regained her composure by time Andy's mother peeked from around the

Regina Puckett

door frame of the connecting room.

Andy went right over to his mother and held up the bags of food. "Look, Mom! Dad and I found work to do." He nodded his head toward Doris. "Mrs. Langford traded some food for us doing yard work for her." He held the bag up toward his mother. "Doesn't that smell good?"

While the youthful chatter was unexpected, the sight of Andy's mother really dumbfounded Doris. The woman had to be well over six feet tall. She didn't appear to have missed very many meals. While Michael had said she was home sick, the woman had the appearance of being in better condition than her husband and son were. While all of these thoughts ran through her mind, she really hoped the surprise and confusion did not show in her expression.

When no greeting came from Andy's mother, Doris indicated the bags of canned goods in her hands. "Where would you like for me to put these?" She didn't add that they were beginning to get heavy. After being on her feet all day from shopping and then cooking, she was just about exhausted.

After staring at Doris for several moments, Andy's mother finally nodded toward the room in which she was standing. While she was a big-built woman, her voice came out as a soft surprise. "You can bring them in here."

Doris had to push past the woman because she only backed up a couple of inches out of the doorway. She didn't even offer to take the heavy bags from Doris, but just pointed toward a rickety table that stood in the middle of the otherwise bare kitchen. There was the usual sink with an odd, old-fashioned woodstove next to it, but there weren't any chairs to go with the table and no cabinets above the ancient-looking sink to store dishes. It was a tiny room, so with the three of them now surrounding the kitchen table, the room was filled to capacity.

Doris placed the sacks of food onto the tabletop. Now that her mission had been accomplished, she was at a loss on what to do or to say next. Fortunately, at that moment, the sounds of the chainsaw starting filled the air, so Andy went into a rambling tale about his dad and Gerald, about how they were going to cut the two fallen trees into firewood so they could use it later for the kitchen stove. While he was doing that,

Regina Puckett

Doris took another unobserved chance to look around the room again. It was amazing to her that anyone could live like the three of them were living in that rundown shack. She could see completely through some of the holes in the outside walls. The place had to be freezing cold in the wintertime.

She had been so busy looking everything over she didn't notice that Andy's mother had focused onto her again. She couldn't stop the blush that flooded her face from the embarrassment of being caught being so nosey about their living conditions.

She stammered, "Would you like for me to help you put this away? I thought since Andy had such a hard day, and I know he has to be hungry, that we might fix him a plate of food while Gerald and Michael are outside cutting up the firewood."

Andy's mother shook her head. "No. We eat together or we don't eat."

The look in the mother's eyes let Doris know that there wouldn't be any more discussion on that subject, so she grabbed the bag with the tea in it. She found the paper cups in another bag and sat them next to each other on the table. "How about a glass of tea, then? The people at church tell me my tea is the best they have ever had."

She watched the silent exchange of Andy pleading with his mother for this one concession to his dad's strict rules. After a moment, the mother finally nodded. "Okay. I don't see anything wrong with that."

Doris poured the tea and gave a cup to each of them. "My legs are tired after standing up all day. Could we go and sit in the living room until they are finished outside? It may take them a while."

Andy's mother tasted the tea and then smiled. "This is good tea."

She looked over at Andy and her expression softened a bit. "Okay. We might as well be comfortable while waiting."

The next few minutes were extremely uncomfortable. The tension in the room was high and with nothing to talk about, Doris sat on a hard, dingy chair and watched Andy and his mom sip on their iced tea. Andy dropped his cup of tea first. Doris watched in amusement as his mother struggled to get out of her chair to go over to him when he followed the glass to the floor. After a moment of tottering between standing and sitting the mother finally fell onto her face too.

Doris stood, dusted any dirt from her pants, and then surveyed her handiwork on the floor. "It's about damn time. I have never had to work so hard for anything in my entire life."

First, she walked over to the mother and kicked her in the side to make certain the woman was out cold. When she was certain that she was, Doris pulled a tiny bottle of super glue from where she had stored it earlier in the day in her pants pocket. She then knelt and applied the glue to the mother's mouth first and then to the son's. After checking to be certain the glue was holding, she went back into the kitchen and rummaged through the bags until she found the roll of cord she had hidden in a Tupperware bowl.

She quickly went about tying the two of them up, like Gerald had taught her how to do when they were first married. Over the years, she had added a few touches of her own. She had been the one to think about using super glue. It came in handy in keeping people from screaming. That was always such a bother when they did that. Even if they weren't in the position of drawing attention to what was happening to them, it was just so annoying, all of that needless racket. It gave her such a headache and it really was such a useless waste of energy. The fact was they were going to die. Why wear themselves out before that happened? Really, just be a good sport and die.

Doris felt bad no one had gotten to eat the good meal she had prepared for them. They had worked so hard for it, but she had offered. It wasn't her fault they kept turning the food down. Gerald's father had said time after time that pride always came before a fall. The thought of Gerald's father always brought a tear to her eye, but there was too much to do to stand around and to think about the good old days.

She looked around the living room. Everything seemed to be taken care of, so she headed outside to help Gerald, but by the time she got there, it seemed like he had everything under control.

"You already have him loaded into the trunk?"

Regina Puckett

Gerald wiped the sweat from his brow and nodded. "The older I get, the heavier it seems they get." He looked toward the house. "You have everything taken care of in there?"

Doris grinned. "Well, of course, dear. Was there ever any doubt? You know I make the best sweet tea around. Just one sip and you're going to drink it all up. Andy may have had too much for his small body though, so maybe we should get everyone loaded into the car before he dies on us. You know how I hate it when the meat spoils. In this heat, it wouldn't take long."

She glanced over at the car and pulled out her container of super glue. "Do you need this?"

Gerald shook his head and pulled out a bottle from his shirt. "No. I bought my own this morning while we were out grocery shopping." He grinned. "I think that's the best idea you have ever had."

She slipped her bottle back into her pocket. "It does come in handy."

She nodded toward the house. "I can carry the boy but it's going to take the two of us to load the mother into the car."

Regina Puckett

She stopped and grinned from ear to ear. "You're going to be so proud of me when you see her. She's huge. She has enough meat on her to last us all winter."

Gerald followed Doris toward the shack. "I hope you're wrong about the boy. I was hoping to just store the three of them in the storage shed tonight. You know our show comes on at seven. I know we can record it, but I'm tired. It's been a hard day."

After going inside Gerald felt for a pulse on Andy. "It's weak but I think he'll survive the night. We won't miss our show after all."

After getting the car was loaded and they headed back to the highway, Gerald began humming. He finally let out a pleased chuckle. "It's just like my daddy told me when I was no older than Andy back there. You put the right bait on the hook and you'll catch something every time."

Doris wiped at the corners of her eyes and sniffed. "Gerald, you know how sad it makes me when you talk about your daddy." She brightened for a moment before saying, "I did add just the right spices with him, though, for lunch. He really did make the best meatloaf."

The End

Regina Puckett

PIECES

Regina Puckett

Kelli slowly became aware of the sound of loud whispers, but she couldn't find the energy or desire to escape from the dark corner into which she had crawled. This safe haven was a place she always used to flee from the harsh realities of life.

Unfortunately, someone was determined for her to resurface into the real world, because they ceased any attempt at trying to be quiet and began using a louder, no-nonsense voice to get her attention. "Mrs. Sharp. Are you awake? Can you hear me?"

After a couple of failed attempts, Kelli finally opened her eyes, but even with them wide open, her immediate surroundings were cloudy and out of focus. She tried blinking to clear up her muddied vision, but that didn't help so she closed them again and kept them that way for a few seconds before trying again. The second time, things were a little clearer but still murky and gray. The only thing she could make out very well was a bulky form hovering off to the side of the

Regina Puckett

bed. She stared at it for a couple of seconds before an excruciating pain in her left temple forced her to close her eyes again.

"Mrs. Sharp!" This insistent command was followed with a jarring jab to her shoulder. "Wake up. We need to talk."

Since there had never been a day of peace in Kelli's life, she wasn't surprised when someone grabbed her shoulders and began shaking. While it might have been his intention to wake her, the movement from the shake made her head rock back and forth, and that in turn sent a jarring pain down her neck and into every single nerve in her spine. It now felt as if her brain might very well explode and gush out of her ears.

One of the many lessons she had learned during her thirty years of marriage to Mark was that there was nowhere to hide if someone wanted to find you badly enough, so in spite of the pain, Kelli forced her eyes open. For some reason, the large form was now leaning in so close, all she could see was another set of eyes staring into hers.

This surprised the person leaning over the bed, enough so that he stepped back and away

Regina Puckett

from the bed railing. With him now back and out of her face, he was no longer a fuzzy blob.

The stranger was a nice-looking man in a rough sort of way. His hair was closely shaven to his scalp. His clothes were rumpled but clean. His nose was long and sharp. That, added with his pointed chin, made for a tough, chiseled appearance. Two bright, intelligent blue eyes were the only things that softened his otherwise hardnosed expression. Even though he was frowning, it was easy to see he usually smiled because there were laugh lines deeply etched into the corners of his eyes.

Kelli and the stranger sized each other up for an unusually long time before he finally cleared his throat.

"Mrs. Sharp. I'm glad you're awake. I need to ask you a couple of questions. There's a killer out there somewhere and the sooner you can give your version of what happened last night, the sooner we catch this madman."

Those words hung in the air between the two of them like nasty darts of acid. Kelli watched them pop around her head and then jab into her

Regina Puckett

brain. Each word attempted to worm its way inside, as if trying to help her remember something extremely important, but in the end none of his words made any sense and all she could do was stare at the man.

She saw a movement on the other side of her bed, so she turned to see what it was. She was pleased to finally see a familiar face. "Sherry? Where am I at? Who is this man and what does he want?" Kelli shook her head to clear her thoughts but stopped immediately when sharp pains reminded her that was a bad idea.

Her daughter reached out and took her hand. "Mom. This is Detective Jensen."

The detective leaned in again. "I'm Detective Jensen. Your husband was brutally murdered last night. A neighbor saw your backdoor standing open this morning and went over to check to see if everything was alright. The moment he saw the blood all over your kitchen, he called 911. When the patrol officers arrived, they found you and your husband out in the garage. I'm afraid there was nothing that could be done to save your husband."

Regina Puckett

Kelli glanced at Sherry. Sherry gave her hand a reassuring pat. "It will be okay, Mom. Just tell the detective what he needs to know."

Sherry then released Kelli's hand and left the room. It was only after the door was closed that Kelli looked back at Detective Jensen. "Do you know what happened to Mark?"

He didn't answer right away but walked over and pulled up a straight back chair closer to the bed. He settled into the chair and then pulled out a small pad and a pen from his coat pocket. He flipped the pad open and began writing before finally focusing on her again. "So you don't remember anything about last night?"

His harsh tone was confusing. She wanted to close her eyes again and shut the world out, but life experiences had taught her that hiding from what needed to be confronted seldom worked for very long. "The last thing I remember was going to bed."

"You don't remember your husband being chopped into tiny pieces? I think that would be something that would be hard to forget."

He glanced away to write something else

onto the pad, then looked up again when he was finished. "Why don't we start with something you do remember? What was your husband's full name?"

Something in Kelli's chest was trying to claw its way out, but she focused on the pad in the detective's hand instead. "His name is Mark Russell Sharp. His friends like to call him 'Too Sharp Mark' because he always dresses so nicely. He likes his shirts and pants to be starched and ironed until the creases are sharp as a knife. It's the way his mom always kept his clothes. He can't stand having a hair out of place."

Detective Jensen propped both hands onto the hospital bed railing and studied her. "So you're saying your husband was a very rigid man." He didn't wait for her to answer. "Your husband ran a tight ship at home didn't he? When we were going over the crime scene, I couldn't help but notice that everything in your house is spotless and in its rightful place. Well, except for the blood around the kitchen sink and the mess in the garage. Let's not forget the mess in the garage."

Kellie sucked in a horrified gasp. "Someone messed up Mark's garage? He doesn't like for other people to touch his tools."

The detective sighed. "You don't get it yet do you? Someone messed up Mark. When we arrived, there were body parts everywhere in his nice and tidy garage. There was no forced entry so if you didn't do it, then you know who did kill your husband. Why don't you make my job a little easier and tell me what happened last night?"

"Mark's dead?"

Detective Jensen stood and leaned over top of the bed railing and made it a point to again position himself just inches away from her face. "He sure is. Deader than dead. Generally happens when your head is chopped off and your brain is sliced into tiny little pieces. Now let's quit playing whatever little game you're playing. You got a bump on the head, but my guess is you got that when Mark realized you were trying to kill him. You are covered in bruises and cuts from the neck down; bad bruises that have been there for some time. It looks like some are just now fading, while others are brand new. Now here's my theory. I'm thinking old Mark liked to slap you around a bit and you got good and pissed off about it. You took matters into your own hands and cut him into

Regina Puckett

pieces. It looks like you used the chainsaw until the blade broke off and then you finished with the ax and power saw. For a man who didn't like for anyone to touch his tools, I'd say you did a lot of touching last night."

He leaned in even closer. "Did it make you feel powerful to be in control for once in your life? You know, it's possible a jury might let you off if you confess and tell them about all of the pain and suffering Mark put you through during your marriage."

She shook her head again. "I don't remember what happened. I went to bed around nine last night. Mark stayed up to watch a show on television. I don't know what happened to him or to me. That's the truth. I went to sleep and I woke up here."

Detective Jensen sat again. He stared at her for a long time before finally getting up and going over to a nearby table. He picked up a large brown envelope and came back to sit again. He pulled out something and then held it up so Kelli could see it clearly. He made a circling motion around the center of it. "This is your husband, Mrs. Sharp." He stabbed his index finger at it as he spoke. "This is him here, here, and even way over there. I think that's his tongue over on the sander, but it's been hammered so flat, I'm can't be a hundred percent certain if it is not."

He stood and shoved the picture into Kelli's face. "Do you see over there by the riding mower? I think that used to be your husband's brain." He shook his head. "I can't be certain about that either because it has been sliced, diced, and chopped so much, it's pretty much just a pile of goo on the garage floor. I see some anger issues here in this photo. What do you see?"

A flicker of something flashed through Kelli's brain and then everything came together as if it was a seamless film of the events from her husband's death. She closed her eyes to shut out the detective's inquiring blue eyes. It was more to give herself time to think than to shut out what she now knew. She finally opened them again and took another look at the photo in Detective Jensen's hand.

"Do you have any more photos besides that one?"

He studied her for several long seconds

before finally pulling out a large stack of pictures.

"Could I hold them for a moment, please?"

She could tell from his expression that he was weighing whether to hand them over to her or not.

He finally pushed them through the bed railing toward her. "Sure. Knock yourself out."

She took her time and studied each photo in order to memorize each and every graphic detail. The room was dead silent the entire time she studied them. She appreciated the detective giving her the time she needed to go over each and every photo. She finally held one up. "Do you see this?"

Detective Jensen leaned in closer and studied the photo she was holding up.

"This used to be his hand; the hand he used to shove me down the stairway. The fall caused me to lose the baby I was carrying just weeks before he was supposed to be born. And this photo, this is his other hand. He used *that* hand to hold me underneath the water until I passed out and almost drowned. I wouldn't have

Regina Puckett

minded drowning so much, if it hadn't meant that I would be leaving my two baby daughters alone with him. I always thought death would be the quick and easy way out."

She tossed that photo off to the side and held up another one. "This is the arm he used to strangle me with every time I didn't get his clothes pressed just the way his mom used to do them."

She tossed that photo away too, and held up another. "This is his head. I took out his brain and diced into it searching for every single piece of me that he stole over the years." She threw that photo into the floor.

She shook her head in dismay. "That was such a waste of time and energy because no matter how much I sliced and diced I couldn't find me in there."

She jabbed her two middle fingertips into the center of her chest. "I sawed out his heart because mine had to be inside of his somewhere. It had to be because it's not in here any longer." She didn't even feel the sharp jabs her fingernails were making as she stabbed in the general area of her heart. She held up another photo. "I cut off this foot for all of the times he kicked me unconscious and left me to die."

A strange smile flicked before she sobered again. "He was always so surprised the next morning to discover he hadn't succeeded in killing me after all. I guess I wasn't as easy to kill as he was."

She flipped through the photos until she found the one she was searching for. "You see this? I worked a long time separating his knee from his leg. That's the knee he used to hold me down with while slicing me with a razor blade. That was a little game he invented about three years ago when the beatings didn't seem to be working on me like he thought they should."

She let that photo drop onto the bed next to her. "I'm surprised our neighbor thought our backdoor being left open was enough reason to think something was wrong at our house, because he never once dropped by to check to see why I was screaming every single night. No one ever came when I screamed, but an opened backdoor attracted attention. That's amazing, don't you think?"

Regina Puckett

She shook her head before finally sorting through the photos again and selecting another one. "Oh, here it is!"

She flipped the photo around so Detective Jensen could see it. "Mark's penis. I must have slipped in the blood and hit my head before I could do anything to it. That's really a shame too, because I had such special plans for it. I can't even remember how many times over the years he raped me, but then he always said it was his husbandly right to do whatever he wanted to me, so maybe in your eyes it wouldn't have been rape either. "

She didn't wait for a response but gathered all of the photos from where they had been discarded. She handed them back, one grizzly photo at a time, but before releasing any of them, she made a point to examine each one again.

It was only after straightening and replacing them back into the large envelope that Detective Jensen stood. "I'm going let you rest now, but I'll be back first thing in the morning with my partner. Tonight, I'll station an officer outside your door."

Regina Puckett

He opened his mouth but then closed it again without ever saying anything. After staring at her for an uncomfortable amount of time, he turned and left without another word.

After the door closed behind him, Kelli pulled the sheets up until they were tucked securely underneath her chin. Strangely enough, her mind didn't dwell on the ghastly pictures but on the blinds on the window. With the sunlight shining through each slat, she could clearly see dust particles floating in the air. Were those particles pieces of her that had broken off and now were trying to escape through the closed window? How many insults and belittling remarks did it take to shatter those pieces off her? It hadn't just been being called stupid and a slut every day, but Mark had drilled it into her head how worthless she was. He had finally convinced her that not even her parents had even loved her. After enduring so much mental and physical abuse, she had become like a robot. Her only goal in life had been to survive for another day and to do everything within her power not to make him angry. She had come to accept that she deserved his abuse. After her daughters had moved out of the house, she no longer had anyone to love or be

Regina Puckett

loved by.

While she stared at the dust particles, the door to the room burst open and a young police officer filled the opening.

"Do you need anything? Detective Jensen asked me to stay here for the night, so just call out if there's anything you need."

The young man didn't even turn when Sherry called out to her from the hallway. "Don't tell them another thing, Mom! I'll get you a lawyer and return in the morning!"

The officer smiled and backed out of the doorway, and the door closed behind him.

Kelli pulled herself up by the railing and shouted loudly enough so her daughter could hear her through the closed door. "Go home, Sherry. Everything's going to be okay. You hear me? Just go home and trust me to do what's best for once."

Nothing happened for a few minutes, but then the officer opened the door again and peered in on her.

Sherry shouted over his shoulder. "Okay,

Regina Puckett

Mom. I'll be back tomorrow. Get some rest if you can."

Kelli could hear footsteps fading away from her room. After a moment or two of staring at her, the officer finally closed the door again. She stayed propped on her elbow for a little bit, staring at the closed door. When she was certain her daughter had finally left, she settled back into the pillow and focused her attention on the slats on the blinds again. Unfortunately, this time, focusing on them didn't keep her mind from what had taken place in Mark's garage. She hadn't lied when she told Detective Jensen about going to bed early. She had been exhausted. It had been a very long week. Every night after work, Mark had found one reason after another to be angry with her. Of course he had beaten her. That was what he did with his evenings. He was careful to keep the punches and kicks to where no one at work would be able to see the swelling or bruises. For a man who always seemed to be so out of control, it was odd how he could control where he focused his anger.

How long had she been in bed when she had been roughly yanked out from under the covers? She didn't know the answer to that, but it

Regina Puckett

had been long enough so that she had already fallen into a deep sleep. Most people would never in a million years understand why being pulled out of the bed didn't surprise her. In her existence, it was not unusual for Mark to continue the beatings after he had time to rest up and make up another reason she should be taught a lesson about something. It could have been something as simple as a piece of lint on the carpet that she had missed when vacuuming. So, when she was pulled out of the bed, she hadn't even questioned what was taking place. It all happened so fast, and before she had even had time to focus, she had been knocked unconscious.

When she regained consciousness, she was lying on the floor of the garage. Her head hurt, but since she was used to being beaten, that fact didn't take top priority. It wasn't until she tried to sit up and realized her legs and feet were duct-taped together that it even occurred to her to be afraid. Mark never tied her up for a beating because it excited him for her to fight and struggle. After looking around, she saw Mark on the other side of the garage. He, too, had been knocked unconscious and was bound with duct tape.

Once it became obvious she had regained

consciousness, someone kicked her in the center of her back, grabbed a hand full of her hair, and then forced her into a sitting position. It was only then two people walked around within eyesight.

"Wake up. You're probably just as interested in what we find inside of him as we are."

Sherry had knelt in front of Kelli and gripped her chin, so she had no other choice but to look at her. "Janet and I decided that since you couldn't bring yourself to kill him that we were going to take care of him for you. He has pieces of us inside of him too. I think it's about time we reclaimed what rightfully belongs to us. Don't you?"

Kelli tried to stand but with her feet taped, it was impossible to move. "Don't do this, girls. He's not worth going to prison for." She held out her taped hands. "Cut this off of me and I'll do it. I should have taken care of him a long time ago. I don't mind going to prison. It couldn't be any worse than living with your father."

Sherry shook her head and stood. "Janet and I decided that if we left you taped up through everything, then the police couldn't pin this on you. Don't worry about a thing. We have everything figured out."

Sherry touched Kelli's cheek. "We're here to take care of you for once, Mom. You have always taken such good care of us. You're the only good thing we have ever had our entire lives. This is our gift to you."

Kelli used every argument she could for them to not to kill Mark, but it didn't take very long for the night to turn into a complete bloodbath. Sadly though, no matter how many body parts her daughters sawed off and examined, they couldn't find any of the pieces that had been stolen from them. When daylight came, the three of them were still just as broken apart and shattered as before.

It was Janet who finally decided that they needed to hit Kelli over the head again so she would be unconscious when the police finally did arrive to the house. Kelli had welcomed the pain and the darkness. It helped to shut out the sight of her daughters' blood-soaked clothes and their disappointed faces.

Regina Puckett

Kelli pushed that image out of her mind again by focusing solely on the blinds and dust particles. Fortunately, she was finally able to drift off to sleep again. Sometime in the middle of the night, a nurse came in and gave her more pain medication. That was enough to help her spend the rest of the night without memories forcing her to relive what had happened. Just as she was waking again the next morning, Sherry and Janet came into her room. Both of her daughters smiled as if nothing was wrong. Janet went around to one side of the hospital bed and Sherry went around to the other side. They both offered her their hands and she reached out and took them. They, in turn, reached across the bed and clasped hands until the three of them formed a circle of arms and hands.

Kelli smiled at each daughter. "We have always had each other. He could never take that away from us, could he?"

Sherry nodded. "The three of us make a whole. I'm the brains, you're the heart and Janet is our soul. We're only pieces when we're apart. Dad knew that and that's why he tried to keep us separated."

Regina Puckett

Janet leaned over Kelli so the two of them were eye to eye. "We can't let them take you away from us. You're the only one keeping us alive. You are the only one we have ever mattered to."

Kelli smiled and held her daughters' hands even tighter. The three of them stayed like that for a long time until Kelli finally sat and pulled herself out of the bed. She walked over to the window and pushed it opened. She then pulled the chair underneath the window. She stepped on to it and then climbed onto the window sill. Once she was there, she held out her hands and helped both daughters up. It didn't take any strength to push the screen out of its frame. The three of them balanced on the window ledge and stared off into the cloudless sky before them. With her daughters on either side of her, she took both of their hands. Sherry and Janet reached in front of her and they too joined hands.

Kelli smiled and in turn made eye contact with each daughter. "Now the mind, the soul, and the heart are together again at last. No one will ever be able to break us into pieces ever again."

The three of them nodded, and then, as one, leaned and fell forward

Regina Puckett

Detective Jensen walked around Kelli's hospital room even though there was nothing there to explain what had taken place the hour before. He finally sat in the chair he had used the previous day when he had questioned Mrs. Sharp. He pulled out his notepad and read everything that had been written in it. Her words still haunted him. He hadn't slept at all the night before, because nothing added up with what the evidence at the crime scene told them, and what she had said about what had taken place during her husband's murder.

He couldn't understand why she had confessed to a crime she couldn't have committed. She had been unconscious and taped. There hadn't been a single drop of blood on her when they had arrived. There was no way she could have taped herself as tightly as that duct tape had been on her wrists, and there were absolutely no fingerprints at the crime scene besides the dead man's. While there was no doubt in his mind that she had wanted her husband dead, there was also no doubt in his mind that she hadn't killed him. What was really driving him insane was the fact that she had committed suicide. Why? Her husband's death had set her free. It was a puzzle within a puzzle.

The door to the room opened and Jensen's partner entered. Tom leaned against the nearest wall and took a quick glance around the room before finally speaking. "The only witness we have is dead, so where do we go from here?'

Jensen slipped the notepad back into his shirt pocket before shaking his head. "What am I missing here? I have more questions than I have answers."

He blew out a long frustrated breath. "She told me about the baby that died when her husband pushed her down the stairs. Why she didn't say anything about her daughters?" He scratched behind an ear. "It's sad to think about losing all three of your children. She had no one she could love or anyone to love her back. I bet you ten bucks he killed her daughters too. Crib deaths, my ass. That evil son of a bitch killed them too. He took everything from her, didn't he?"

Detective Jensen stood. "I'm surprised she didn't kill herself sooner, and I personally don't give a damn who killed Mark Sharp. That man can rot in hell, and I hope he's there this very minute, trying to find all of his damn pieces."

The End

Regina Puckett

PAYING THE HITCHHIKER

Regina Puckett

Susan heard the car pulling up before actually seeing it. A moment earlier, she had been considering repositioning the too-tight, sweat-soaked thong, but since there was now an audience, she pasted on her sexiest smile and then crossed one leg in front of the other. For some reason guys couldn't resist that stance. She arched her shoulders and then leaned forward just enough so her ample cleavage peered out from the edge of the tank top's neckline.

The truck's electric tinted window purred as it lowered. Its opening revealed two men in their late twenties. By their grimy appearances, it looked as if they might be just returning home from a hard day of labor. The passenger took off his baseball cap and a greasy layer of dirty blonde hair fell across one of his thick-skinned droopy eyes. That look on any other man would have looked sexy as hell, but it only served to make him creepier.

"You need a ride?" His voice sounded as if he had just swallowed bits of broken glass and

Regina Puckett

sawdust. His wide smile revealed a dental nightmare of three chipped teeth on the top and a series of missing teeth on the bottom. The jerk winked and unlatched the door as if assuming she couldn't possibly pass up such a great offer. When he leaned forward, his weight on the door popped it open a couple of inches. "Jump on in here and settle yourself between me and Tommy. We'll take you where you need to go." That statement was followed with both men exchanging a look that could only be described as unsettling.

Susan waited long enough for them to return their attention back onto her before sighing in disgust. She instantly relaxed the seductive poise and straightened her posture so her cleavage was no long visible. "I'm heading to California. You guys going that far?"

The driver leaned forward and cradled both arms across the top of the steering wheel so he could see her from around his traveling companion. He wasn't missing as many teeth as his friend, but the expression on his face sent a shiver all the way through her spine. Before saying anything, he gave her a total, lingering body scan. "You jump on in here and I'll take you places you have never been before." If that implied innuendo wasn't disgusting enough, he jabbed his friend in the side, and both of them broke out into laughter as if that was the best joke either one of them had ever heard.

For Susan, that was the final straw. To put a stop to anymore lewd suggestions, she reached into the handbag hanging off of her shoulder and pulled out a small handgun. Without blinking an eye, she aimed it just inches away from the passenger's head. "The smartest thing the two of you can do right now is to put your truck in gear and move on along. I'm going to California. If that's not where the two of you are heading, then I'm not getting into the truck with you."

She motioned the gun toward the front of the truck. "Get out of here now before my finger gets all hot and sweaty and I accidentally shoot you. Shooting either one of you wouldn't bother me in the least, but I would rather not spend all night explaining to the cops why I killed you."

Neither man moved a muscle, but both eyed Susan as if trying to decide if she was serious or not. When the gun never wavered from the passenger's forehead, he put on a brave face and spit out a wad of a repulsive brown substance

Regina Puckett

which fortunately missed her feet by about two or three inches. When he saw her look of disgust, he gave a self-satisfied grin. It must have been a big enough victory for him, because he finally slammed the door shut. Although that seemed like a good sign that they were going to leave, they didn't. They continued staring at her as if sizing up just how serious she was about shooting one of them. It seemed as if they might be considering doing something stupid, so she clicked the hammer back just to prove the point that she was deadly serious. The moment that click reverberated through the still-hot July air, the driver jammed the truck's gears and punched the gas. Gravel and soil went flying into several different directions.

As the men drove off, Susan waved furiously underneath her nose to try and stave off the gritty dust. It took a couple of seconds for it to settle, and when it finally did, it was a relief to see the truck's tail lights disappearing out of sight. Feeling almost certain they weren't coming back any time soon, she placed the gun back into the shoulder bag and went about straightening her ponytail and dusting off her clothes. While she was busy doing that, another vehicle slowed and pulled

Regina Puckett

up beside her.

This time a tidy, semi-attractive lady in her late thirties leaned out of the passenger window. "You look hot and tired. Where you headed to?" Her voice had a nice southern, musical tone that was very charming.

By this time, Susan's thong was tucked somewhere deep inside of her nether regions, and sweat was dripping all the way from her hairline down to the waist band of her slacks. She was too hot and tired to mask her irritation and she didn't bother striking another sexy poise. She did manage to smile after a couple of deep breaths. "I'm going to California. The two of you wouldn't be heading in that direction would you?"

The tiny brunette grinned and motioned toward the backseat. "It's your lucky day! That's exactly where we're going, and a little company would be nice."

Susan bent over to get a better look at the driver, but the moment she did, the passenger popped out and blocked her view. When Susan scowled, the woman backed away enough for Susan to see into the car. The driver was staring

Regina Puckett

out the front window as if he was uninterested in what was happening between them, but after Susan stared at him for several minutes, he turned around and made eye contact with her. He turned out to be just as mousy and unassuming as his companion. It didn't take long for him to turn back around as if the entire meeting was something he could either take or leave.

"That's my husband, Jason." The lady extended her hand as if expecting a formal introduction. "I'm Jennifer O'Hara. I can see that you're a little nervous about getting in the car with two complete strangers, but we really are heading out to California. Jason's mom and dad live there. His dad was in the Air Force and when he retired they decided to stay out there since they both loved it so much."

When Susan didn't take the offered hand, Jennifer lowered it and relaxed against the side of the car. "We haven't seen Jason's parents since our wedding last year. We both have two weeks of vacation so we thought this would be a great time to do a little sightseeing on our way out west. Neither one of us put much thought to how boring all of this nonstop driving was going to be, though. It really has just been so tedious. Once you've seen

Regina Puckett

one corn or wheat field, then you have pretty much seen them all."

Jennifer stopped talking only long enough to fold both arms across her chest and briefly look Susan over from head to toe. She then cleared her throat and smiled again. "We've been on the road all day and were beginning to get tired of talking to each other. It would be great to have a third person to chat with."

She shrugged one shoulder before jamming both hands into her jeans pockets. "We're really very boring people but harmless. I promise that you'll be safe with us." She leaned forward a bit and whispered dramatically. "Jason's not much of a talker. He's more of a man of action if you know what I mean."

Susan glanced over toward Jason to see how he was taking being discussed as if he wasn't even there. When he finally noticed her staring again, he turned and shrugged. As soon as that little bit of communication was over, he turned and peered forward again as if he was used to his wife's nonstop chattering.

Because the man seemed unconcerned

about whether or not she accepted the ride, Susan finally nodded. "Sure. I appreciate the lift."

Both women climbed into the car. Jennifer returned to the front passenger seat, and Susan slid into the backseat. She stretched both legs out across the seat and settled in for a long ride. She reverted into a sitting position, when without any explanation, Jason pulled into a parking lot of a rundown motel.

Susan looked at him and he returned that look in the rearview mirror.

For the first time since stopping to pick her up Jason broke his silence. "Jennifer and I have been on the road all day. I'm just stopping for a quick couple of hours sleep before heading back out tonight. Why don't you and Jennifer run across the road and pick up some sandwiches and something cold to drink? I'm exhausted."

His smile was brief, but there was something in it that was reassuring. "You don't mind do you? Jennifer doesn't drive and this will be the first time I have been able to rest all day. I promise to be back on the road as soon I catch a couple of hours sleep."

Regina Puckett

In spite of her best judgment, Susan nodded. The women stayed in the car while Jason checked in. When he returned, he moved the car into the farthest parking space away from the office. If the motel wasn't disturbing enough on its own, because of its dilapidated appearance, the fact that their car was the only vehicle in the large parking lot was enough to send a feeling of dread down Susan's spine.

As soon as the engine shut off, Jason reached into his back pocket and pulled out a wallet. After fishing around in it for a while, he handed Jennifer a couple of twenties and a few ones. "The two of you pick up what you want to eat and drink. Dinner's on me. I'll probably be asleep by time you get back to the room. I'm so dead tired you're not going to disturb me, so watch television, eat, or even take a short nap while you're waiting."

Jason unlocked the trunk of the car and pulled out a couple of black suitcases while Susan and Jennifer headed across the busy highway toward a small mom and pop grocery store. They wandered the store's aisles for about thirty minutes with both of them throwing in items into the food cart as the impulse struck them. Jennifer chatted and giggled nonstop. It didn't take long to accumulate an odd assortment of chips, cookies, fried chicken, and other unhealthy snacks.

The longer Susan stayed with Jennifer, the less uneasy she was about the short stay at the motel. Jennifer and Jason were a little unorthodox but otherwise seemed to be a fairly harmless couple. She certainly understood unconventional people. One of her mother's famous sayings to her was that she had a bad habit of flying by the seat of her pants. Susan personally hated boring and unoriginal people. Let everyone else get caught up in the rat race and go to their nine to five jobs every single day of their lives. That regimen wasn't ever going to be for her. She didn't want the two point five kids or the husband who only came home when it was convenient. She loved her freedom and every so often met some interesting people. So what if her lifestyle was slightly dangerous? She had her carrying permit, a pistol, and an entire box of bullets.

True to his word, Jason was sound asleep by the time they returned. He was covered head to toe underneath the hotel's ugly flowery bedspread and he was snoring to beat the band. While Jennifer was setting their odd assortment of food on the room's small table, Susan took that opportunity to use the room's tiny bathroom. It was an enormous relief to be able reposition the uncomfortable thong and to wash the dust and grime from her face and hands. She swore she hadn't been in the bathroom more than a few minutes, but by the time she came out of it, both Jennifer and Jason were standing on either side of the bathroom's doorway waiting for her.

Jason had Susan's gun pointed about chin level at her, and his mousy face had taken on a very distinct hardness she would have never thought possible for him to pull off. Her gut reaction was to bolt back into the bathroom and lock the door, but it seemed as if Jennifer already had that move covered. She had her body positioned in such a way that even if Susan had been able to shut the door, Jennifer would have been shut in there with her. The two of them struggled over the door knob until Jason was finally able to position himself in such a way he could press the barrel of the gun against the side of Susan's head. With that accomplished, he cocked the trigger and everyone halted as if someone had pushed the pause button on a VCR.

"What are you going to do with me?"

Regina Puckett

Jason stepped back just enough so the gun was no longer pressed against her head. It was still only a few inches away from her face. In a weird sort of way though, while that didn't make the pistol any less deadly, it didn't feel quite as threatening.

Jason motioned the gun toward the nearest double bed. "We have loads of plans for you. I could take the time to name them all off but that would be wasting precious time. I think it will be more fun to let all of our games be a big surprise. Don't you? Now be a trooper and go lie down like a good girl. Just don't try any funny stuff and everything will be okay." He added a wink as if she needed more clues as to what the surprises were going to be.

Susan took her eyes off of the gun only long enough to peer lower. From where she was standing, it didn't look as if everything was going to be okay.

When she didn't move, Jason pointed the gun up against her forehead. "You haven't been making very good decisions today now have you, Susan? I think now would be an excellent time to just do as you're told. I can promise that if you do, then this will be the best decision you have made all day." He slid the gun all the way from her forehead to the middle of her chest. He eyed what tiny bit of cleavage was peering out from under the edge of her tank top, and if that wasn't unnerving enough, he licked his lips and grinned over toward Jennifer. "You sure know how to pick em, baby. She's the best one yet."

Mentally, Susan was freaking out, but since it seemed as if she didn't really have any other choice in the matter, she did as instructed. Pushing past Jason, she walked over and sat.

Jason smiled and nodded. "Good. That's good. Now lay face down in the middle of the bed. If you do just as you're told to do we'll all leave this room a little happier and wiser for the experience."

When Susan didn't move as quickly as he thought she should, Jason made another threatening motion with the gun. That was enough to make her scoot toward the center of the bed and turn over until her face was pressed in between the center of the two pillows at the head of the bed. The bedspread smelt like mildew and something too gross to think about. Because the smell was so awful, she breathed through her mouth in the hopes that would lessen the stench some. Once she was situated, Jennifer climbed onto the bed next to her with a roll of duct tape in one hand and a pair of scissors with the other. She straddled Susan's back and then sprawled on top of her.

While Jennifer wasn't heavy, the extra weight was enough to push Susan's face further into the dusty bedspread. She tried not to gag and it took every ounce of control she had not to buck up and toss Jennifer off of her back. Since she wasn't exactly certain where Jason was standing, and if he still was holding the gun, she didn't want to make any sudden moves that would startle him enough so that he accidently shot someone. He didn't seem to be the brightest guy in the world, so she remained still and waited to see what was going to happen next.

It didn't take very long for Jennifer to make her first move. She pressed her cheek on top of Susan's and let it lay there for what seemed like a long time. She then drew in several long breaths as if she was trying to memorize Susan's scent. When she finally pulled her face away, it was just enough to look into Susan's eyes. "We're going to have so

Regina Puckett

much fun with you. I wanted you to watch, but Jason's shy, so I'm going to have to put a pillow case on your head, for now, until he's more comfortable with having you in the room with us."

She leaned in closer and licked the side of Susan's face. "Don't worry. I bet I can talk him into to letting you watch later. Right now, it's just enough that you're here with us. First, I'll talk him into letting you watch and then we'll see about letting you join in. After watching us, you'll be ready to enjoy the games we play." Jennifer licked Susan's face again. "We're very good at them. We're so good you won't even remember we had to hold a gun on you in the beginning."

That set Jennifer into a weird set of giggles and then without warning, she stuck her tongue into Susan's ear. When she sat up, she spoke with a teasing and flirty tone. "Sorry about you missing your dinner, but if you're a good girl, I'll feed it to you myself later. Would you like that?" Without waiting for an answer, Jennifer reached over, grabbed the nearest pillow, and yanked its case from it. She gently lifted Susan's head and slid the case over it. When that was done to her satisfaction, she pulled Susan's arms behind her and duct taped her wrists together. As soon as everything was secured to her liking, Jennifer rolled off of her. "Isn't this the most fun you have ever had?"

Susan could feel the bed bounce as Jennifer climbed off of the bed. The noises that could be heard next sounded as if Jennifer suddenly took off running across the room. She must have then dived straight into Jason because he grunted. He must have dropped the gun because the next sound was something heavy plunking onto the carpeted floor. For the next hour or so, all Susan could hear was giggles, groans and bodies slapping together. It was like being in the room with a porn movie you weren't watching but to which you were listening. It would have been easy to doze off if she hadn't been so uncertain when the insane couple was going to get tired of coupling like dogs in heat and suddenly decide to include her into their activities.

With every breath a little of the pillowcase was sucked into her mouth. The material soon had her mouth dry and it was making it even harder to breathe since the pillow case's thick material wouldn't allow much air through. The smell of the inside of the pillowcase was even worse than the bedspread. It was hard to decide if it smelled more like rancid body odor or three-day-old piss. Sadly enough, it could have very well been a mixture of both since the motel was in such a sad state of disrepair. If it had been up to her she would had rather been outside in a sleeping bag than this crumbling, mold-infested dump. It was hard to believe that this was how far her life had fallen.

The hardest thing to accept was that her mother had been right all along. She really did fly by the seat of her pants too much. How could she have been so stupid to leave her purse with two complete strangers? She never did that. She had fallen for the oldest con in the world. They had seemed to be two sweet people, so she had just thrown her purse onto the bed when she had gone into the bathroom. It hadn't seemed like such a big deal at the time. Jason had been snoring as if asleep and Jennifer had busy on the other side of the room putting the food out.

It had always been a hard and fast rule for her never to let anyone else touch her gun. She had been careless and stupid to trust these people. Living with her dad should have taught her every dirty and low down scheme in the world there was to know. You never trusted anyone with your money, body, or weapons, and you always screwed someone before they screwed you. He had certainly done that to her in more ways than one during her lifetime.

Susan had been so busy chastising herself she didn't realize for a moment or two that all of the earlier noises of lovemaking were missing. For some reason she found that more unsettling than having the bed slapping against the wall and all of the grunting and groaning accompanying it. Maybe the two of them were so exhausted from all of their game playing they had fallen asleep. That thought had no sooner passed through Susan's mind, than the pillowcase was suddenly removed. She blinked a couple of times before finally being able to focus on Jason.

The expression on his face was disquieting to say the least. He flicked the end of her nose as if the two of them were in a bar and he was flirting with her. "Jennifer has talked me into it."

He grinned and waited for a reaction. Susan shook her head in the hopes of clearing away some of the fogginess. Because her mouth was so dry, she had to run her tongue over her teeth to separate them from her lips before she could speak. "She talked you into what?"

Regina Puckett

He flicked her nose again. That action was very annoying because it was making her nose itch.

"We want you to watch us now. You'll get a kick out of it. If you're a real good girl, we'll let you join in the next time."

"The next time? Damn. What's wrong with the two of you? You've had enough sex to kill the healthiest people in the world. I'm exhausted and I have just been lying here the entire time."

He climbed onto the bed next to her, leaned in, and breathed heavily against the side of her neck. He smelled strongly of sweat, sex, and corn chips. It was enough to turn her off of chips for a very long time.

"I can be talked into letting you join us now if you want to. It sounds to me as if you have been over here missing all of the fun. I'm so sorry. We've been so inconsiderate of you."

He turned to his wife. "Go get the scissors. She wants to join in on the fun."

Jennifer jumped onto the bed on the other side of Susan. "I told you! I don't know why you always have to be talked into this type of stuff."

Susan could hear the scissors behind her and could feel the tape being cut away. While Jason was busy doing that, Jennifer leaned in and licked Susan's face again. "I told you. If he had agreed earlier, you wouldn't have had to be taped up and just waste the whole night away over here by yourself. I bet it has just been killing you to hear us over there and you not being able to join in."

She pushed the hair out of Susan's eyes and then caressed the side of her face. "He can be such a fuddy-duddy sometimes. It takes me forever to get him to do what I want him to. I don't know why he has to play so hard to get when he knows all of my ideas are so deliciously wonderful."

The moment the tape was off of her hands, Susan pushed Jennifer off of the bed onto the floor. When Jason tried to grab her shoulder, Susan shoved him backwards. In one quick movement, she jumped off of the bed and ran over to where she had heard her gun hit the floor earlier. As soon as it was back in her hands, everything felt more in control. When she saw that Jason and Jennifer weren't going to try and challenge her, she tucked it into the waistband of her slacks. With that taken care of, she flipped her ponytail off of her shoulder. First she glared at Jennifer and then at Jason.

It would have been so easy to shoot them both for all of the discomfort they had caused her over the past couple of hours, but fortunately for them, the cell phone in her back pocket rang before that idea could settle and take hold. When she was pulling it out to answer, Jason moved in her direction. She held up one finger to stall him and gave him a glare that would have turned most men into stone. Fortunately, he was smart enough to stop in his tracks and wait.

Susan pressed the phone up against her ear. "Yeah."

Her mother's nasally voice barked through the phone. "Where the hell are you? If you don't get to the next arranged pickup before the hour is up, you're going to miss your client."

Susan glared at Jason and Jennifer again. "Well, tell that to Mr. and Mrs. O'Hara here, and while you're at it, be sure to charge them extra for

Regina Puckett

going over an hour. You can also charge them for duct taping me. Didn't you explain to them that bondage would be extra? Next time go over the entire contract with them. You should have explained about having to pay for all of the extras. This was just supposed to be a simple 'picking up the hitchhiker and having me watch them have sex.' I didn't even get my lunch out of the deal like I was supposed to."

"Get your panties out of a wad and just get to your next pickup point."

Susan pulled at the thong through the material of her slacks. "That's another thing. I'm not wearing any more of these torture devices. I would rather not wear any underpants at all then to have to go all day with a piece of thread jammed up my ass."

Her mother snorted. "Just get to your next pickup and quit complaining in front of the customers. We need their repeat business. You think people with hitchhiker fantasies just grow on trees? And about your underwear, if you had been doing your job right, they would have already been off by now."

Regina Puckett

With that said, all Susan heard next was silence, so she clicked the end button and turned toward the O'Haras. "We went over on the time so now I'm running late to my next client. Would you mind running me over to Haynes Street? I don't think it's too far from here."

Now that they were off of their sexual high, they looked a little shamefaced for keeping her tied up for so long. They scurried around the room to gather all of their belongings while Susan went back into the bathroom to try and clean up a little before her next appointment. This time, though, she carried her purse and gun in with her just in case the couple decided they liked playing "Kidnapping the Hitchhiker" a little too much and decided to do it for real.

By the time she came out, Jason had already taken the suitcases back out to the car and Jennifer was gathering all of the food together they had purchased earlier. The moment Susan stepped out of the bathroom Jennifer held up the container of fried chicken. "It's cold but you could grab a bite to eat before you head out."

Susan shook her head. "Thanks, but I'm in a big hurry. You ready to go?"

Regina Puckett

Jennifer grabbed the grocery bags and nodded. "Yeah. This place is a dump. Jason only chose it because no one ever stays here, and we knew we could make as much racket as we wanted to and no one would be the wiser." She grinned. "He isn't much to look at but he certainly is a stallion in bed. Next time he won't be so shy and we won't have to put a pillowcase over your head."

They left the room together and then climbed into the car.

Susan relaxed into the headrest on the back seat. She tried to refrain from sounding like a school teacher. "About that. You know all of those little things like bondage and me joining in on the sex games cost extra, so work that out with my manager before we do this again."

She leaned forward and jabbed Jason in the shoulder with the end of her finger. "And next time don't touch my gun. Shit like that will get you killed. I didn't know if we were still playing your fantasy games or it was for real. Fortunately for the two of you, I'm a good sport and I went along with it, but I thought seriously for a minute about taking it away from you and blowing your brains out."

Regina Puckett

She leaned back into the seat again, while they both had the grace to look nervous and more than a little spooked. "I enjoy a freaky time just like you do but let's understand the rules right up front, and next time, I'll show you the best time you ever had. It will be an experience you will never forget. I can promise you that it will better than having me all tied up on another bed all night. I didn't even get to watch any of the action. From what I could hear, the two of you were having fun. You two are animals."

Jason grinned over at Jennifer and it was easy to see that her earlier remarks about the gun were now forgotten. Jennifer figured they were already calculating how they were going to be able to afford her services for more fun. To reel them in, she leaned toward the front seat and toyed with the back of both of their necks. "I know what. Instead of me playing hitchhiker why don't we pretend I'm selling cookies to buy a new cheerleading uniform?"

Susan watched them both squirm under her expert touches. She even tickled Jennifer's ear as an extra bonus since the woman seemed to like playing around with her ear so much. She figured it must be a very sensitive area for her. It

Regina Puckett

appeared as if she had hit pay dirt because Jennifer began wiggling in her seat.

Jason turned in his seat. "Do you have a cheerleading uniform to wear? I love cheerleading uniforms."

Jennifer giggled. "I do, too. I really do. How about next Friday night? I think we have enough money in the bank to pay for an entire weekend."

Satisfied that she had done her job to retain another set of returning customers, Susan sat back. Damned she was tired. "Sounds like a date. Call my manager with your credit card number. Be sure to include the extras this time. You have to ask for full sexual contact or all I can do is watch. I know. It sucks but I have to follow the rules just like my clients do. It doesn't matter how much I want to join in on the fun. I can't if it hasn't been included in the deal. You guys have been loads of fun, though. I'm looking forward to next Friday. I think I even still remember a few cheers. There's nothing like doing a couple of backward flips and the splits to get the juices flowing."

She looked at her watch and groaned. "I'm

Regina Puckett

going to be so late."

Jason cut the headlights on and backed out of the parking spot. He caught her eyes in the mirror. "It's kind of late to be standing out by yourself on the side of the road. Haynes Road is hell and gone from anywhere."

Susan shook her head. "I'll be fine. That's where this couple likes to pick me up. They chose that area because there aren't many cars on it, and no one will see them picking me up there. I'll be fine. Besides if someone tries to cause me any trouble, I have my pistol."

Jennifer turned in her seat. "I'm sorry about the gun but as we were pulling up next to you this afternoon I noticed you putting it back into your purse. Jason didn't want to use it but I thought it would make the game more exciting and it did." She closed her eyes and shuddered. "It really is exciting to have so much control over another person." She reached over and tugged on Jason's ear. They grinned at each other and sighed.

Susan tried not to gag at their puppy dog expressions.

Fortunately another thought occurred to

Jennifer, so she turned her attention back to Susan. "So does this next couple get excited about picking up hitchhikers too?"

Susan shrugged. "Not really. They don't have any children. They like pretending they see a lost girl on the side of the road. They pick me up and Effie cooks me this huge meal. She makes me take a shower and she washes my hair and combs it out for me. While I'm sitting by a fire drinking hot cocoa, she washes my clothes for me. I spend the night and in the morning, she has an enormous breakfast cooked. When I'm finished, they take me home. It's their thing. They want someone to take care of and they like me. It's the best full night's sleep I get all week."

"Really? Don't you think that's a strange fantasy?'

Susan stared at Jennifer. This chick was really asking her if she thought someone cooking and cleaning for her was strange, when they had just spent the better part of two hours holding her hostage and having sex in the same room with her tied up in the bed next to them. What was the proper answer to something like that? She didn't have one, so she shrugged. Fortunately, they

Regina Puckett

arrived at Haynes Road so she didn't have to discuss Howard and Effie anymore.

Susan slid out of the backseat. "See you next Friday." She leaned forward to reveal as much cleavage as possible. "My uniform is blue. It's the same color as my eyes." She held her fingers just where her legs and hips meet. "It's about this short. You'll be surprised what you can see when I jump. Maybe I'll be able to make up a cheer just for the three of us." She reached back into the car and traced a finger along the edge of Jennifer's ear. "Until next week."

The taillights for the O'Hara's car disappeared around a curve just as the headlights for the Smith's truck appeared coming from the opposite direction. Susan was looking forward to a quiet night with the sweet couple. Dealing with people's sexual fantasies was really beginning to take a toll on her. Even just pretending to play like a lost girl for the Smiths was getting to be old. She had been playing so many different roles for so many different people she was beginning to lose sight of who she was. There had been a time when she had dreamed of going to college and making something out of herself. Here she was at twenty-three and she felt old and broken. Maybe it was time to get out of this lifestyle and use the money she had earned to move off to another state and finally realize her dream of becoming a nurse.

Susan was surprised when the Smith's truck stopped and Howard was by himself.

"Hey. Where's Effie?"

The older gentleman reached across the cab of the truck and opened the passenger door for her. "She's at home. She was fixing a special meal for you and wasn't completely finished with it yet. I hope you don't mind riding with an old man tonight all by yourself. You know how Effie is. She's not happy until every little thing is perfect."

The moment Susan had her seatbelt on he grinned and whispered dramatically. "Don't tell her that I told you but I think she was throwing a peach cobbler in the oven as I was leaving."

Susan squealed like a three-year-old and clapped. "That's my favorite. I love you guys. I gain five pounds every time I stay with you two."

They chatted nonstop all the way to the Smith's farmhouse. In a lot of ways the old couple felt more like family then Susan's own screwed-up parents ever had. They didn't have a child and they really wanted someone to love. Her parents had someone to love and they used her as a commodity to be sold to the highest bidder.

Thinking about her parents had Susan depressed by the time she entered the cozy kitchen. The smells coming from the oven were heavenly.

Susan pulled out the nearest kitchen chair and sat in it. "Where's Effie?"

Howard scratched the stubble on his chin and looked thoughtful. A second later, his eyes lit up. He snapped his fingers. "She said something about having a surprise for you in the barn."

Susan couldn't stop from sighing. She was tired, dirty, and hungry. The smells in the kitchen were too enticing to leave but these were paying customers so she had no choice but to look excited by whatever game they wanted to play. As she trudged alongside Howard toward the barn, she silently wished with all of her might that Effie wasn't standing out in that barn naked. That would just be the final straw tonight. There was nothing worse than getting your taste buds all worked up for a good hot peach cobbler and then discover you had to miss eating it in because you had to watch some old couple have sex.

When Howard opened the barn door the first thing Susan noticed was a terrible stench. "Whoa! What smells so bad?"

He looked puzzled for a moment before answering. "Oh, yeah. I guess I'm used to it by now. My old hound dog died a couple of days ago. I put her out here until I have the time to bury her. Effie and I have been out back in the woods all week cutting up firewood for winter. I guess I forgot about old Sam."

Susan looked at him. "You really can't smell that?" She pinched her nostrils together with her fingers and breathed through her mouth instead. It seemed like it was going to be a day filled with horrible smells.

"So where's Effie and this big surprise at?" No sooner were those words out of her mouth than Effie jumped out from one of the stalls. She was carrying one of the largest chainsaws Susan had ever seen. Before Susan could ask why she was carrying a chainsaw, Effie pulled its cord and

Regina Puckett

it rumbled to life. The air in the barn filled with a jarring sound, fumes, and smoke. Just having Effie jump out of the stall was starling enough but the larger than life running chainsaw was too much. Without giving it a second thought, Susan pulled the pistol out of her purse and shot Effie in the middle of the forehead. Everything after that happened in slow motion. Effie actually stood there for a stunned second before her brain shut down and she fell. Her finger didn't immediately release the trigger on the chainsaw so it was still running as she fell on top of it. It sawed into half of her torso before it finally grounded to a halt. Without it running, the barn was now deadly silent.

Both Susan and Howard looked at Effie's body for a moment before looking back at each other. When she saw the look on his face, she turned the gun toward him.

He opened his mouth a couple of times before finally being able to get the words out. "Why did you do that for?"

Susan nodded toward the body and chainsaw. "She had a damn chainsaw. What did you think I was going to do, just stand here while she whacked me into tiny pieces? I don't get paid that much."

He waved both hands in the air as if trying to pull his words out of the air. "It was joke. She thought it would be funny. She would jump out and scare you. We would all laugh and then go in and eat peach cobbler."

Susan shook her head and spluttered. "Who thinks jumping out with a running chainsaw is a joke? That's crazy thinking and I know crazy. I live with crazy every day and that shit's crazy!" Her voice rose each time she said the word crazy until the last word came out as a shout.

Howard turned as if to leave the barn. "I have to call for help. Effie needs help."

Susan took a step forward. "Stop right where you are. You're not calling anyone."

Howard only stopped for a moment before heading toward the door again.

Susan jumped closer to him. "I'm sorry." She shot him in the head until there were no more bullets in the gun. She looked around at the mess in the barn that hadn't been there a couple of

Regina Puckett

minutes earlier. Why had she thought the night was going to be better than the morning had been? That seldom happened in her life.

Her brain finally snapped out of its haze. She did what she usually did in these types of situations she pulled out the cell phone and called her mother.

"Hey, Mom."

Susan listened to dead silence for a moment and when her mother finally did speak, she sounded groggy. "Did you miss your ride? Don't tell me that you missed your ride. The Smiths are going to want their money back. Do you have any idea how much they pay me every week to be able to take you home with them? If I have to give that money back, you're going to pay twice that amount back just for waking me up and pissing me off."

Susan was finally able to get a word in when her mother stopped her ranting. "I didn't miss my ride and the Smiths aren't going to want their money back."

"Why are you calling me so late then? You only call me when you've screwed something up."

Regina Puckett

Her mother paused and then groaned. "You killed them didn't you? Why do you have to kill every client we have? I tell you and I tell you not to kill them. You know clients don't grow on trees don't you?"

Susan jumped into the conversation again before her mother could get going again. "They had a chainsaw. I thought they were going to kill me."

Both women were silent for a moment. "I'm not even going to ask you why you thought they were going to kill you. What's done is done. What do you want me to do? You know in the end I'm always going to have your back, but you're working twice as much next week to pay me back for all of the trouble you've caused me tonight. First, you're late for your appointment and then you go and kill your best customers. Real businesses are not run like this."

Because Susan needed mother's help, she didn't bring up all the ways she didn't have her back. "Bring the gas can and some matches. This old barn looks like it wouldn't take much to burn it down." She paused to think if she was going to need anything else. "Oh, yeah. Bring me some comfortable underpants. This thong is killing me."

The End

Regina Puckett

INHERITANCE

Regina Puckett

"I might as well say goodbye now, before my phone loses its signal. Someone really needs to put a tower in these hills." Since the last turnoff from the major highway, the secondary road was harder to navigate because it was narrower and extremely curvy. Accalia needed both hands on the steering wheel, so she pulled the phone away from her ear long enough to tuck it between her ear and shoulder. One wrong move and she could easily lose control of the car.

Caleb's voice was difficult to understand over the static. "I hate that you're not going to be here for your birthday. It's not every day that you turn twenty-one."

Accalia raised her shoulder to press the phone against her ear. "No big deal. We'll celebrate as soon as I return next weekend. I hope you plan on being the designated driver though, because I'm going to enjoy all of the benefits of finally reaching the legal drinking age."

She waited for Caleb's reply, but after several seconds of only hearing dead silence, she let out a frustrated groan and tossed the phone into the passenger seat. "That's it, I guess. No more communication with the rest of the world for seven days."

It wouldn't have been so bad if her grandmother didn't keep refusing to have a phone installed in the old farmhouse. Not only was Accalia unable to call anyone when she visited, but every time her granny needed to make a phone call, she had to drive over to the nearest neighbor or into town to use the payphone. It was becoming even more worrisome because of her grandmother's advanced age and the isolation of the farm. Accalia couldn't help but worry that something bad might happen and her grandmother would not be able to make the trip to the neighbor's house or into town. It would be days before anyone would think to go check on her, but the woman was far too stubborn for her own good.

Now that weren't any distractions besides the curvy, narrow road, Accalia had plenty of time to think about the last phone conversation with her grandmother. The entire tone of it had been very troubling. There had been a weird undercurrent of something her grandmother had seemed to want to say but hadn't. Since she never asked for anything, Accalia agreed without hesitation to take a week's vacation. After all, making the trip seemed like such a small thing to do in exchange for making her grandmother happy. She owed her so much since she had been the one to raise her after her parents' deaths.

To stop that train of thought, Accalia focused on driving on the uneven dirt road. The next road was in worse shape and harder to navigate. It took every bit of concentration to watch out for the deep ruts and holes. In several places, it was rutted so badly the bottom of the car scraped against the dirt. That nerve-racking experience lasted for a little over thirty minutes before she was finally able to make the turn into her grandmother's long drive. To say it was a drive was really upgrading it. It was more like the hint of a pathway between trees and bushes, but it could have been much worse. It could have rained recently, but fortunately, that hadn't happened in several days.

Soon the trees had the path so narrow and almost impossible to steer through. Low hanging branches were now scratching the top of her car while the underbrush scratched at the paint on its sides. The thick canopy of leaves all but shut out any sunlight. It was a creepy place in the middle of the day and not a place you wanted to be at night. Even though Accalia had played in these woods while growing up they still were kind of spooky. There was always the feeling of having something or someone watching you.

It was a relief finally to drive out of the woods and into the clearing surrounding her grandmother's house. As if sensing Accalia was close by, her grandmother opened the front door and waved. Accalia waved back. Seeing her grandmother's smiling face made her smile There was something about visiting home that made her feel complete.

The house needed a fresh coat of paint, but it was still a charming sight. Inside of the low picket fence, the yard was neatly mowed and the flower gardens were free of weeds. Even though her grandmother was in her mid-seventies, she could still outwork most men. While she no longer used the hundred plus acres to plant crops for resale, she did still grow a small garden for her own personal use. The older lady was a strange combination of stubborn pride and a loving, nurturing spirit.

Accalia left all of her belongings in the car and ran to her grandmother. She threw both arms around her neck. "Granny! You're looking well."

Regina Puckett

Her grandmother wasn't the most demonstrative person in the world so while Accalia was hugging her, her grandmother self-consciously pat her on the back and patiently waited for the hug to end.

When Accalia finally released her, her grandmother nodded toward the opened door. "Come on in. I have a nice pot of tea brewing. We'll catch up before you bring your things in." She pushed a long strand of unruly brown hair out of Accalia's face. "I have missed having you around the place so much. It's good to see you."

The tears in her grandmother's eyes took Accalia aback. She pulled her into another tight hug. When she pulled back, Accalia cupped her grandmother's face between both palms. "You okay, Granny?"

Her grandmother sniffed, but she nodded. "Don't pay any attention to this old fool. I was thinking about your mom and dad the other day and I had to see you." She linked her arm through Accalia's. "Come on in and let's have that cup of tea."

They sat at the kitchen table with not only the promised tea, but a large slice of chocolate cake in front of each of them before her grandmother spoke again. "Are you still seeing that nice young man Caleb?"

Accalia swallowed a bite of cake before answering. "I am. He wanted to come with me but he couldn't get out of work for an entire week. He just took a week off not too long ago to go home and see his parents. He really wanted to come, though." Just thinking about Caleb made her smile. "He's so sweet. He's taking me out for my birthday when I go back home next weekend. It's getting pretty serious between the two us." She looked back down at the slice of cake before asking her grandmother the next question. "Did you like him?" When she looked up again, she saw a frown on her grandmother's face, but she quickly replaced it with a smile when she saw Accalia looking.

"He seems nice enough. He's a little too ambitious for my liking, but the world has changed a lot since I was out looking for the perfect man to fall in love with and marry." She reached over and patted Accalia's hand. "Besides, it doesn't matter what I think about him. You have good instincts so I trust you will find the ideal man."

Her grandmother put her napkin on the

table and pushed her chair backwards. "I was wondering if I could get you to fetch me something out of the basement? I have a box of things I would like to give to you, but it's too heavy for me to carry up those steep stairs."

"Sure." Accalia stood and walked over to the basement door with her grandmother. She looked at the bottom of the door before opening it. "What happened to the door?"

Her grandmother gave a dismissive wave and shrugged. "It's a long story. I'll tell you after you find the box and bring it back up."

Accalia didn't argue, but before heading downstairs, she eyed the long, narrow section that was missing from the bottom of the huge wooden door. She couldn't even begin to imagine why her grandmother would have had a section of the door cut out. It was too small of an area to use for anything. However, she had learned years ago that when her grandmother had made her mind up about something, there was no changing it. The only way she was going to find out why the door had been cut was to go downstairs, get the box, and bring it back upstairs.

"Okay. Where's this box in the basement? I didn't know you were keeping anything down there since the time you discovered rats had taken over that area."

Her grandmother seemed not to hear her but opened the door without answering.

"The box?"

Her grandmother wrung her hands together. "What?"

Accalia tilted her head and looked at the worry lines around her grandmother's mouth. She reached over and touched her arm. "You okay?"

Her grandmother nodded, but there was a thin layer of sweat on her forehead. "I'm fine, dear." She motioned at the stairway. "The box is in the back corner by an old mattress set I took down last summer."

That comment was enough to raise Accalia's eyebrows without any effort on her part. She wanted to ask why her grandmother was lugging a mattress set down those steep stairs without any help but she didn't. She cleared her throat instead. "Okay. I'll be back in a minute. Don't throw my cake away. I'm going to finish it when I get back up here with your box."

Going down the steep staircase took concentration and nerves of steel. Accalia had to hold onto the walls on each side of the steps to keep her balance. She had always hated the basement. It wasn't a very pleasant place. It had always had a strange, gloomy feeling to it. There were strong, dark feelings of being trapped in the damp, dim room. About halfway down, her arms broke out in goosebumps, and a sudden feeling of dread crept into her pores.

One of the reasons the basement was so creepy was because there were only two lights for the entire large area. One was located in the center of the stairwell and the other one hung from a long cord in the middle of the basement ceiling. They were both bare, low wattage bulbs that didn't give off enough light for the room. All they really did was cast eerie shadows everywhere, leaving all of the nooks and crannies in the dark. When Accalia reached the center room, she turned in circles. There wasn't a single object anywhere to be seen. Not believing her own eyes, she walked around the edges of it again just to be certain she wasn't wrong.

Regina Puckett

She did that a couple of times. When she was back in the center of the room, she looked at the wooden floor. It appeared to have been swept recently.

After another quick look around the empty room, Accalia walked over to the bottom step and looked up toward the doorway. She had expected to find her grandmother waiting there for her but instead all she could see was a closed door at the top of the stairs. A brief flash of panic shook her to the core, but she managed to tamp that down and then chastised herself for being such a ninny. How could she have forgotten so quickly how conservative her grandmother was with electricity? She had shut the door so the cool air wasn't wasted on the basement area. How many times, while growing up, had her grandmother told her to shut a door or turn off a light when leaving the room?

That realization calmed her racing heart to some degree, so she took a deep breath and headed back upstairs, but when she reached the top and tried turning the knob, it refused to budge. Her heart rate rose again but instead of going into a full-blown panic, she calmly knocked on the door. "Granny? There's nothing down here. Open the door. It's locked." She knocked again and waited.

Regina Puckett

After what felt like an eternity, she heard her grandmother shuffle over to the door. Accaila released the door handle and waited. When she didn't hear the lock being turned she knocked on the door again. "Granny."

Finally, after not receiving an answer, something was slid under the door to her. When she looked down, there sat a saucer with a slice of chocolate cake on it.

"I'm sorry but this has to be done. You'll thank me later."

Accalia stared at the cake and waited for something to make sense. She knocked on the door again. "Granny?" The only answer to that was the sound of her grandmother shuffling away from the door.

Accalia was too stunned to move. She stood with her hand poised in the air for at least a full ten minutes, as if she was going to knock again, before she finally realized her grandmother wasn't coming back. With nothing else to do, she sat on the top step, wrapped both arms around her knees, and stared off into space. She waited without any clear thought as to what she was waiting for. She flipped

Regina Puckett

through each and every absurd possibility, but no matter how she looked at her situation there was nothing to explain it. Finally, after spending some time there with nothing to do but think, she thought of one possible answer. Maybe her grandmother was going to throw her a surprise birthday party. Locking her in the basement was a crazy way to get her out of the way. She was definitely out of the way now.

After deciding that a birthday party was in the works and all she had to do was to sit out her exile, Accalia picked up the saucer of cake. "That's got to be it." She eyed the cake. "Granny could have at least given me a fork." She let out a long, frustrated sigh. "This is the craziest thing she has ever done. I hope she's not going senile." She picked up a bite of cake between two fingers and stuffed it into her mouth. She chewed and wished she still had her cup of tea. "I'm going to kill her when I get out of here." She took another bite and spoke with her mouth full. "I really am going to kill her when I get out of here. She knows I hate dark places and she knows I especially hate this basement."

It didn't take long after finishing off the cake to become bored with just sitting around, so she stood and banged on the door again. After several minutes, Accalia finally heard her grandmother outside the door again.

"Accalia Renee Anderson, you stop beating on the door this instant! You're giving me a terrible headache."

Fearing her grandmother would leave again, she called out. "What's going on, Granny? Why have you locked me in here?"

She didn't hear anything for a moment and then heard her grandmother walking away. A few seconds later, she heard the sound of a chair being pulled over to the door. For a while, there weren't any more sounds until her grandmother began speaking. "I'm sorry to do this, but it was the only thing I could think to do."

Accalia waited for her to finish explaining herself but when she didn't, Accalia leaned her forehead on the door separating the two of them. "But why, Granny? I don't understand."

"I have to tell you something about your family. I guess I should have a long time ago, but the time just never seemed right."

Since it seemed like this conversation was going to take a while, Accalia sat on the top step again and leaned her back against the closed door.

"I'm hoping the curse will skip you. I have always only wanted a normal life for you." Her grandmother paused but after a brief time resumed. "I don't know how many generations the inheritance and curse goes back."

The term "inheritance" made Accalia sit up and pucker her lips together. Nothing her grandmother was saying made any sense. What inheritance and curse? Her earlier unease returned in full force, but before she could ask any questions, her grandmother continued speaking.

"I wanted you here before your twenty-first birthday because if it's going to happen to you, it will be then. I went ahead and locked you in the basement because sometimes the change can come earlier than on the day of your birth. You were a couple of days late so it could happen on the day you were supposed to be born. I just couldn't take any chances that it would and that you wouldn't know how to control it. You could accidentally hurt someone before you learned how to control it on your own. I know you're certainly smart enough to

Regina Puckett

figure it out, but we live in a day and age where people shoot first and then ask questions later."

It was quiet again for a moment. "Do you understand what I'm saying to you?"

Accalia leaned her back against the door again. "No. You're speaking in riddles, Granny. What are you talking about? What change, curse or inheritance. Why would someone shoot first and who on earth would I hurt? You know I would never hurt a fly. This is crazy. Let me out of here so we can talk face to face."

For a long time there was only silence and then finally there was the sound of the chair being moved again. After a moment or two everything settled down again. It was only then her grandmother cleared her throat. "I wish I could. I didn't want to lock you in the basement. I know how much you always hated going down there after it became infested with rats, but it was the only place I knew you wouldn't be able to break out of later. You have no idea how strong you will be, and I needed you locked up before we talked. I knew if I didn't do that first, you would just think I was a crazy old lady and leave before the change. If nothing happens on your birthday I'll let you out, but not before then."

Regina Puckett

Accalia played with the now empty saucer while she tried to process the latest bit of information. The more her grandmother talked, the less Accalia understood.

"Let me out and I promise I won't leave. There's no point in us having to have this talk with a locked door between us." Accalia waited a moment before adding. "You know I have always done everything you told me to do. Why wouldn't I do that this time too? I promise to not go storming off."

Accalia held her breath and prayed her grandmother would finally listen to reason, but was soon disappointed.

"I'm sorry, dear, but I can't let you out. It would be too dangerous for you and for everyone else."

Accalia slammed the saucer as hard as she could against the edge of the top step. The fragile china broke into tiny pieces but in that instant, she didn't care she had broken one her grandmother's favorite pieces of china. She stood and pounded on the heavy oak door with both fists. It really served no other purpose than to release the overwhelming frustration that had been building up from the forced imprisonment.

She didn't even try to mask her rising temper this time. "What are you talking about? This is stupid. Let me out of here right now! If you don't open this door this instant, I'm never coming back here again."

Instead opening the door, her grandmother pushed something else through the opening at the bottom slit. Accalia reached down and picked up a sealed plastic bag. Because of the dim lighting, she had to hold it up close to see what was in it. It appeared to be some sort of cereal or trail mix.

"What's this?"

Instead of an answer, she only heard the sound of the chair being pulled back away from the door. After the sound of wood scrapping against wood stopped, Accalia heard her grandmother shuffling back toward the door again. Her voice had an uneven quiver in it. "I'm not feeling well. This has been even more stressful than I thought it was going to be. I'm going to go lay down and I'll be back to talk to you later when you are more willing to listen to me." No sooner was that said, than a loud thud sounded against the door. Then, there was the sound of something sliding against the door.

Accalia stood with her ear pressed against the door as if that would help her discover what was happening on the other side of it. "What's wrong, Granny? Are you okay?" The oppressive atmosphere seemed to become heavier with each second that passed without an answer. With no other options to left, Accalia knelt on the steps and tried to see if she could see anything from the cut of slit in the bottom of the door.

At first, she couldn't make heads or tails out of what she was seeing, but she finally realized she was looking into her grandmother's eyes. "Granny?" She repositioned herself so she could get a better view, but no matter which way she turned, the view stayed the same. Even after staring for several minutes, her grandmother never blinked her eyes.

Accalia asked her grandmother time after time if she was okay but no matter what she said or asked, her grandmother never responded or blinked. Accalia must have stayed in that position on the steps, staring through the slit for over an hour before the truth finally sunk in. Her grandmother was dead and she wasn't going to be unlocking the basement door for her. She began trembling from grief and the horror of her situation. "Granny! Granny! Please get up. Please don't leave me here. Please don't leave me alone. Please, please, please!"

Accalia stood. She had been in that same cramped position for so long, she was now stiff and clumsy. When she tried standing, she swayed backwards and almost toppled down the stairway, but fortunately, she caught herself in time.

With so many thoughts rushing through at one time, Accalia couldn't settle on any one long enough to come up with a plan. Since she was halfway down the steps, she headed back down to see what her options were. Each step downward was like voluntarily walking into hell. Once into the room, she circled it several times before finally running both hands along each wall, searching for a hidden door. It was a futile waste of energy because all of the walls had been built from stones and mortar. No matter how many times she pried and prodded, nothing budged. The only exit was the locked door; the door her grandmother was now lying in front of, dead.

Accalia leaned her forehead against the stone wall. She swallowed back the bile that was threatening to spew out. After several deep cleansing breaths, she let out a hysterical giggle. "I'm stuck in a bad Edgar Allen Poe story. Any minute now, my alarm clock is going to go off and I'm going to wake up. I'll tell everyone at work about my horrible dream. We'll laugh about it, go out, and buy a nice juicy burger for lunch. None of this is happening. I'm turning twenty-one in three days."

In spite of repeating this over and over, the roughness of the stone biting into her forehead was a stark reminder that she was not asleep and she really was stuck in the basement. She began crying, because there was no doubt in her mind that she was going to die down there. "Caleb's taking me out to celebrate. I have so much I want to do. Please, God, don't let me die down here."

She had a small bag of trail mix and no water. She didn't have any idea how long it took to die from thirst but no one was going to be looking for her for at least another seven to nine days. It might take even longer than that if Caleb thought she had decided to extend her visit.

At some point, Accalia stopped thinking but walked in circles around the room. She touched and kicked every inch of the room in an almost primal need to find a way out of the room. There was nothing rational in the way she went about her search. She would kick one stone and then run to the opposite wall and kick another stone. After several hours of running from wall to wall and stone to stone in a total panic, she finally collapsed in the middle of the floor and curled into a tight ball. She cried and screamed until her eyes were dry and her throat was raw. At some point, she finally dozed off. That didn't bring any relief because she dreamed of her grandmother chasing her around the room trying to tell her something, but every time she would start talking, Accalia would cover her ears and refuse to listen.

When Accalia finally woke up, she climbed the stairs again and tried looking under the cutout slit to see if her grandmother was still there, but it was now pitch black in the kitchen and it was impossible to see anything. She sat on the top step, opened the plastic bag of trail mix, and nibbled on it but her throat hurt from the earlier screaming and crying so she resealed the bag. She was going to sit the bag on the step when her hand brushed up against a piece of the broken china. She picked it up and decided to try to use it on the door handle, but the only thing she accomplished with it was a few scratches on the wood around the doorknob. She gave up after stabbing herself the back of her hand. The wound was very superficial but it sent her into another fit of crying. To stop herself from screaming again, she sucked on the cut and tried to staunch the blood flow. By the time the cut had stopped bleeding, she had snot and tears running down her face so she used the hem of her blouse clean it off. With that taken care of, she tried looking under the edge of the door again, but she still couldn't see anything so she went back into the basement to go over every inch of it again.

Accalia walked and crawled around every square inch of the room time after time. Each hour merged into the next. She would doze off when she became too exhausted to do anything else and the moment she woke up again, she started the entire process all over again. The hours turned into days. She only knew that time hadn't stopped completely because of the times she would climb up the steps to look under the door at her grandmother. Even though each day made the sight almost too much to take in, she couldn't stop from climbing the stairs time after time to look just to make certain that she was really locked in the basement and she wasn't stuck in a nightmare.

Nothing changed in her routine until darkness had filled the kitchen the night of her twenty-first birthday. By this time, her mind was already slipping in and out of rational thoughts. The searches were becoming less frequent and the time she stayed asleep was now consuming up most of her days and nights. Even though she still made the trip up the stairs, she now had to crawl up the stairs with regular rest stops along the way.

The trip that night resulted in her becoming dizzy and falling. She was too weak to move, so she stared at the light bulb over the stairs until a series of stabbing pains coursed in and out every nerve of her body. At first, she tried curling into a tight ball but when she tried, her body began writhing in horrible spasms. Each pain forced her body to contort and shake. It took grim determination to force herself up onto her knees and palms. She swayed in that stance for several seconds before a pain shot through her as if she had been electrocuted. She fell back to the floor with so much force it knocked her unconscious.

The next morning, Accalia found herself curled on the top step of the stairs and every inch of her body ached. It took her a few minutes to sit upright and when she was finally able to focus on something besides her aches and pains, she stared at her hands. Her nails were ripped and ragged. The ends of her fingers were a bloody mess. She rubbed her hands together and tried to work out the stiffness. When that didn't help, she turned to look at the door. Running from top to bottom of the door there were now deep scratches. In several places there were splinters sticking out and in many places there were entire chunks of wood missing. The dirty white paint was covered in streaks of dried blood.

Accalia was in too much pain and too thirsty to think so instead of wondering about what had happened the night before she turned around and wrapped both arms around her knees. She rested her head on the top of them and rocked. The slow motions helped to ease the pain. It was in that position images began flashing in and out behind her closed eyelids. It was like seeing scenes from a bad horror flick. She tried squeezing them out by forcing her eyelids together even tighter but that didn't help. Soon the images were joined by the memory of scents.

None of these made any sense. The only explanation for the images and scents had to be from remembering a nightmare. There were paws and claws scraping at the door, and then an animal trying to force its nose underneath it, trying to smell the decaying corpse of her grandmother. This animal had even tried to snap at her grandmother's face in an attempt to eat the flesh. All of this was accompanied with a consuming feeling of primal rage and frustration.

Accalia would have cried but she was too exhausted to attempt it. She did manage to whisper through her parched and painful throat. "I'm not crazy. I'm not crazy. Please God; tell me I'm not crazy."

Although she did not think she could cry, a lone tear escaped the corner of one eye. It went unnoticed as it ran down the side of her face and into the collar of her blouse. She tried to hum her favorite song, but stopped because of the pain. Instead, she closed her eyes, rocked back and forth and sang the words in her mind just to keep from thinking about anything else.

After a few days, Accalia didn't need to look underneath the door at her grandmother to know she was still there. The sounds of the flies that were now covering her grandmother's body were all she needed to reassure her that yes, her grandmother was indeed dead, and that soon enough Accalia would be joining her. The next three nights were just another repeat of the first painful nightmare. Pain would wrack her body until she was unconscious. The next morning, she would be curled on the top step with the same images to try to force out by trying to remember something good from her life. She thought about Caleb more and more. She focused on him and their love. It was what kept her from giving up and begging God to let her die.

Accalia no longer tried going down the steps into the basement. She stayed on the top step with her back to the door. There was no doubt in her mind that if she ever made it down, she would never have the energy climb them again. The funny thing was she no longer noticed the stench coming from the other side of the door. It was just part of her hellish existence. It was one of the things that kept her grounded and how she knew for certain that she was still alive.

When the sounds first started, it wasn't as if she hadn't heard them but she figured they were just part and parcel of the hallucination thing that had taken over her existence for the last several days. She had imagined being rescued so many times that when the door opened she didn't even bother looking up, but kept her face pressed in the curve of her knees.

"Accalia?"

She didn't even turn when someone touched her shoulder. It wasn't until Caleb said her name again did she turn to look at him. She wanted to smile but her lips were too dried and cracked to work, but inside she smiled. Inside, she did a back flip and a cheer, while the rest of her fainted.

"More flowers?"

Caleb moved a vase of roses over so he could fit the newest flower arrangement onto the table nearest her. He then leaned and kissed her forehead. "There aren't enough flowers in the world to let you know how relieved I am that you are okay."

He sat on the edge of her hospital bed and took her hand into his. "How are you feeling today?"

Accalia raised her arm in the air. "No more

Regina Puckett

tubes running in me. I can't tell you how excited I am finally to be free of all of that. It was a trial pulling the stand, bags of fluid and tubes over with me every time I had to go to the restroom and I won't bore you with what I had to do to take a shower and wash my hair."

    Caleb kissed the back of her hand. "I'm just so happy you are here to complain. I thought when I opened the door I was too late to save you. I can't even begin to imagine how much you suffered in that basement. I still don't understand what your grandmother was thinking. Do you think she had dementia? She couldn't have been in her right mind when she locked you in there."

    Accalia covered her eyes with her forearm and tried not to cry. It was too hard thinking about her grandmother lying there for so long before she could be buried, and she hated what people were saying about her. The news had been filled with such awful stories about her being locked in the basement. The media had taken the story to the airways as soon as Accalia had been rescued. The whole sordid affair had been analyzed from every direction. It wasn't the ending Accalia wanted for her grandmother. She had lived a good life and had only done wonderful things for other people during that lifetime. She didn't deserve what was happening now, but Accalia had been too sick to defend her and it had all happened without Accalia there to protect her good name.

Accalia uncovered her face and looked Caleb in the eyes. All of the love she felt for her grandmother sounded out with each word. "Granny didn't mean for this to happen. I'm certain of that. She was worried about something. I never understood what. She said something about an inheritance and a curse. It had something to do with something before her father or she had been born. She might have finished telling me if I hadn't thrown such a fit and demanded that she let me out right then. She became so stressed over me not listening to her that she had a heart attack."

Caleb kissed the back of her hand. "Now stop that. You didn't cause your grandmother to have a heart attack. It was her age. The next thing you'll be saying is it's your fault she locked you in the basement. You're getting out of here tomorrow and in a few days I'm going to cook you a big meal to finally celebrate your twenty-first birthday."

When she opened her mouth to protest, he

shushed her. "I'm not going to take 'no' for an answer. It's time to put all of this behind you and get on with your life."

He leaned forward and kissed her on the lips. He then leaned his forehead against hers and they sat like that for several minutes before she realized there was something different about him. "Perfume. You smell like perfume."

He sat back. His eyebrow drew together in confusion. "Perfume? What are you talking about?"

She smiled and shrugged. "I don't know. It seems like my sense of smell has become more sensitive since I have been here. You smell like perfume."

Caleb lifted his shirt collar and sniffed. "I don't smell anything." He then snapped his fingers and smiled. "I know. Connie stopped me on my way out of the office and asked how you were doing. I told her I was on my way over here, so she hugged me and told me to tell you to get better soon. I bet that's it. She always wears too much perfume. No one has the heart to tell her how offensive it is to everyone else."

Regina Puckett

Accalia stepped onto the elevator and pushed the button for the thirteenth floor. As soon as the doors closed, she leaned against a wall and waited while it traveled the short distance to Caleb's floor. She still wasn't fully recovered, but she had made up her mind to try to return to doing normal everyday things so her life would begin feeling as if it belonged to her again. There were still moments she flashed back to being in the basement. She always tried to think about something else as quickly as possible so those memories would go away. Most days she was successful, but other days she couldn't block out everything.

There were times she could almost remember being in another form. There were recollections of moving differently and thinking differently. It was as if she had been in a form that operated on instinct rather than rational thought, but then she guessed when a person was on the verge of dying they went to a different sphere of existence.

She couldn't help but look at her hands. Her fingers were still in the process of healing and her fingernails didn't look as if they were ever grow back to be the same. She wondered what she had

Regina Puckett

done those last four nights. Her fingernails made her think of those images of having paws and claws. They were the reason she examined the thoughts of trying to sniff out her grandmother's corpse in order to try to grab some portion of her grandmother's face with her teeth to try and eat it.

Accalia shoved her hands into her pockets and focused on the lights blinking as the elevator traveled from floor to floor. She was relieved when the doors finally opened and she had something else to do besides wait. She focused all of her attention on the ugly beige carpet in the hallway. It was easy to lose the bad images when Caleb opened the door and smiled. She loved his smile.

"Come in. I have your meal favorite in the oven. I know how much you love roasted chicken." He took her arm and nudged her toward the living room sofa. "Sit. I'll be right back. I'll throw the dinner rolls in and everything will be ready to eat."

He kissed the end of her nose. "You look good." He smiled again before heading back into the kitchen.

Accalia basked in the warmth of that smile and that kiss for several seconds before realizing that she smelled the scent of that perfume again. She stood and wandered around the living room sniffing everything. The room was filled with it. It was on every piece of furniture in the living room. She followed the scent into Caleb's bedroom. She walked over to his bed, picked up one of the pillows, and sniffed. She tossed it back onto the bed, leaned over the bed, and was consumed with the scent of Caleb's co-worker's perfume.

Something flipped inside of her. Her entire body stiffened and in an instant, the same excruciating pain came over her that she had felt in her grandmother's basement. She tried to fight but nothing she did could stop the wave upon wave of muscle spasms. It finally became so unbearable that she fell onto the bed. She tried stifling the groans and in the process bit through her bottom lip. Fortunately, she blacked out before the worst of it struck.

It wasn't that Accalia didn't hear the door being unlocked, because she did. All of her senses were heightened. She had actually smelled the two men the moment they had walked off the elevator and onto the ward. She had heard all of their conversations as they had gone about their nightly duties of dispensing medications and giving the needed shots.

Even though she could hear them heading toward her room, she didn't move out of her crouch. She was in the middle of the room and focused on a spot on the wall directly in front of her. She didn't stare at the wall because there was something interesting there to look at, but looking at nothing freed up the other senses so they could do their jobs. So when the two men stopped outside her door, she waited and listened.

"She's a pretty thing. What's her problem?"

Even with a locked door separating them, Accalia could smell traces of beer and a woman on the man asking the question. There was also a faint scent of fear creeping into his pores while he stood there staring in at her.

Accalia heard the other man's joints move when he shrugged. This man's scent was less offensive. "What do you think? She's crazy."

The other man snickered. "Even I knew that.

Regina Puckett

I mean why is she locked in here by herself. She doesn't look so bad. What did she do?"

"Which planet have you been living on? This is that crazy lady who has been all over the news the last couple of days. You know. The one where they found her on top of her boyfriend eating him? We need to take extra care when we go in there. She probably thinks she's an animal or something. Who knows? This place is filled to the brim with nuts. What's one more?"

The other nurse laughed again as he was unlocking the door. "I'm not worried about this one. She couldn't weigh more than ninety pounds soaking wet, but if you're scared, you can wait out here."

Accalia heard the other man shrug again. "Go for it. I'll watch from out here. If you get in trouble, I'll sound the alarm."

"You're a real piece of work aren't you? All scared of a tiny thing like her. I'll go tweak her ass for you just to show you that she's harmless."

He paused before turning the knob. "Why don't you finish the rounds on this floor alone? You

Regina Puckett

can come and get me in about twenty minutes. It's pretty dead tonight. I'll treat you to a nice meal later. All you have to do is go do your job. You don't have to know what happened in this room if anyone ever asks."

There was a moment's hesitation on the other man's part but even from where Accalia was at she could smell his repulsed reaction, but that wasn't enough to keep him from finally agreeing. "You're really a sick bastard. I don't want any part of this. Go on in there and get yourself killed for all I care. The world would be a better place without you anyway.

Instead of being offended, the male nurse just laughed. "You know this job sucks. I don't see anything wrong with a few fringe benefits. Go on. Get out of here, but don't forget about me later. Remember dinner's on me."

The door opened and then closed but Accalia didn't move or even look in the nurse's direction. She waited on her prey to come to her. She did finally lift her nose slightly as he moved nearer. Out of the corner of her eye, she saw him lay her meds on the bed. Only then, did he move over and stand

Regina Puckett

directly over her.

"You are a tiny thing aren't you? I like them tiny." He lifted a long strand of her brown hair and rubbed it between his fingers. He finally knelt so he was eye to eye with her. It was only then she made eye contact with him. She could smell his arousal so she leaned forward to get a better smell. "You like a good sniff, huh. I'll give you a good sniff. Here, how about this?"

He moved even closer and rubbed himself against her knee. She didn't move or break eye contact. She wasn't concerned about what he was doing because at that very moment the spasms were coursing through her body again. There was no doubt what was going to happen next. Soon she would lose consciousness and her inheritance would do what it was meant to do. It would save her.

▪▪▪▪▪▪▪▪▪▪▪▪▪▪▪▪▪▪▪▪▪▪▪▪▪▪▪▪▪▪▪▪▪▪▪▪▪▪▪

The End

Regina Puckett

ABOUT THE AUTHOR

Regina Puckett lives Tennessee with her husband of forty years. She has been writing for since the seventh grade. Her first love was writing romances but has since branched out to horror, children's picture books, and inspirational short stories.

Printed in Great Britain
by Amazon